Scott Palter

Dead Night of Space
Volume 1
The Hybrid Crew
©Final Sword Productions LLC, 2018
ISBN: 978-1-938339-36-3
By Scott Palter
Content Assistance from: Markus Baur
Other Assistance: Mike Rohde, Duane Oldsen
Editing: Jennifer Seiden Sadler
Layout and Cover: Sam Pray

The Hybrid Crew

Jump Pilot/Navigator – Holly Kim. Visible age, 30. Actually 100+ (her story changes depending on her mood and how many drinks she's had). Currently, she's a somewhat-muscular redhead, but she has played with looks, body types, etc. for as long as her crewmates on *Eagle Totem* have known her (30+ years). Jump navs and pilots are crazy (who else but a nutter could stay awake through the mental chaos of jump space?), but she's extreme even for that breed. She's on this mission because she rolled for it with *Nantucket Prime's* jump witch and lost (neutral dice, as both were known cheats). Didn't want to go and has been a complete pain about it every nanometer of the way and every microsecond of their stay stationside getting the ship fixed. She's good at what she does, but is known to take chances when the whim strikes her. Signed onto *Eagle Totem* off a freighter they stopped and boarded. Ship was real hinky even by Far-Beyond -Shady Merchanter standards. Stories about her past are so wild as to be absurd, mutually contradictory and vague in the extreme on checkable details. Bright, mercurial, manipulative. Degenerate gambler on leave (no one on her ship will play against her). The type who goes on stationside leave with a knife in her boot. Always manages to find the worst dive on any station and the most unstable characters in it. Any leave where she only has to get bailed out of station brig once is a good one.

In-system Pilot – Ben Redson. Twenty-three (actual, not just appearance). He's got a spacer's lean body type and a media star's good looks. Normal personality is shy and quiet. Sit him in a pilot's seat and he's a different person. Reflexes of a cat. His ability to handle 3D-maneuver problems on the fly is off the charts. Natural tinkerer's ability on machine repair. Machines LIKE him. His vice is VR games that challenge his reflexes and situational awareness. When pushed, responds with aggressive male belligerence.

Has zero idea of how to finesse problems or people. Signed on *Nantucket Prime* four years back from some minor system vaguely in Fleet Space. Little formal education. He can barely read and higher math is beyond him. Had been a cargo pusher-turned-asteroid miner. Lots of hands-on experience. REAL ignorant about how the universe works. Knew he wanted deep space (and knew even more he wanted out of his nowhere life in a nowhere system). Doesn't talk much about his past, but there's something about quarrels with his mother and a dead GF. Had another partner die on him in a mining misadventure. Girls hit on him. So do guys. Unlike most in-systemers, he has some experience dealing with both planetary atmospheres and gas giant-skimming. Again, he doesn't know theory, just a lot of hours' experience. Can sit any non-Jump station on a ship except captain or comm—he hasn't the personality for either.

Tech/Armscomp – Elizabeth Windsor [nickname "Winnie"]. Age 37 (actual and visible). Fleet Marine. Got abandoned stationside by her carrier in some classified action. Never managed to catch up with it as its location and missions are often classified. Former rank, Gunnery Sgt. Ran boarding parties and stationside strong-arm ops. Competent fighter with power armor or unassisted. She's a small-repairs kind of tech. Not much for theory, but she enlisted/got press ganged at 14, so she's worked on virtually every sort of ship's equipment and is good at make-do parts and jury-rig repairs. She is also wise to the ways of suppliers and checks every part herself before it gets installed. Been on *Eagle Totem* for six years since she transferred over from a cruiser. Cruiser did routine patrols and it bored her. When bored, she knows how to make trouble for her watch officers without ever quite violating regs. They were happy to see her go (the swap was for a case of supposedly Old Earth single malt plus a few kilos of kitchen spices).

The Hybrid Crew

Tech – Scantech – Katanga Wa-Benzi. He's 66 (looks 35). Wrestler's body but a watchmaker's hands. Features are African; hair, East Asian. Where does he come from? He tells maybe a dozen mutually contradictory stories. Pick one. Maybe it's true. Signed onto *Nantucket Prime* in a stationside bar 20 years back. Station records had him entering on a ship they'd never heard of, claiming a homeport way beyond the Beyond (in other words, either it was from the absolutely farthest reaches of the Diaspora, or the ship's ID was a fairy tale that the ship didn't see the need to make plausible). Katanga has earned ratings on every bit of major equipment his ship carries. He also got certs for the theory behind the equipment. He isn't as hands-on as Winnie or as intuitive as Ben, but he could probably redesign a ship from scratch. His specialty is IT. Hardware, software, interfaces—the damned tech loves him and he loves it. Has homebrew upgrades on every piece of software they have. Can hack most station security systems. He's very good and knows it. He's also very private. No one knows why he wanted to sign onto a Fleet ship. He keeps a social distance from his shipmates. Not hostile—just aloof and indifferent. Whatever drummer he marches to, only he can hear the music. The shipboard joke is one station call he'll just vanish the way he appeared. Indifferent to rank and almost equally so to pay. No one has a clue to which way he swings or even if he is into sex at all. No visible vices beyond spicy food. His crewmates think he's a plant, but cannot agree if he finks for Fleet Security, Fleet Intelligence, the Sector Commander, or some pirate operation. He laughs at all four possibilities. Depending on the day, he will admit or deny it.

Fixer/Communicator/Comtech/IT/nominal Captain/cat-herder – Bridgit Finnmark. Looks 35. No one knows her real age. Has been with the ship since its launch (or so the records say, but records do lie; crew regularly fudges their log entries and presume past crews did the same). From her various expertises, she may have been at some point both a Merchanter and a captain of a large Fleet ship. She can make a crew work together, make impossible missions work, and seems to have a sixth sense on when to sweet-talk and when to strong-arm outsiders. Sector Command seems afraid/ in awe of her, but no one in either crew has details. Can sit any seat in combat. Can probably do any job shipboard except jump witch (those are born not made, or so the folk wisdom goes—no one really knows how or why jump works). Her vices are random sexual encounters (either sex will do) and occasional overt sadism when she has some fool in her power. She's blown up stopped ships simply to work off a mood. Holed a station once that way. She's fine, however, in real combat.

Prisoner – Aagney Ruiz [or so the Fleet ID he showed said; ID looks right, but a ship as small as *Nantucket Prime* can be spoofed]. Seems to be early 30s. Aagney had what appeared to be valid recognition code words and wanted a ride. Seemed indifferent as to where, as long as it got him off the station he was on. Won't say why he wanted off that badly. Won't say his rank or state his business. Seems content to be locked in the brig between meals. However, when allowed out he plays excellent chess, decent bridge, and abysmal poker. Cannot bluff for shit. Still, he wasn't carrying much in gold or jewels to wager. No one trusts electronic money off an unknown. Offers to play for work hours, but that means letting him run loose and no one trusts him that far. He has a planet dweller's heavy body type, but beyond that seems ordinary Earth stock. DNA scan says all primate, but not all human. Will not rise to the obvious cracks about being a chimp. His DNA, prints, etc. do not match ship files of Fleet personnel, but everyone knows those files are incomplete and frequently decades out-of-date. Guy is willing to make small talk, but seems to have no need of social connection. If ignored, goes back to his cell.

Chapter 1

Ben Redson was vaguely coming out of trank sleep from jump when he suddenly became aware of the klaxon. He had been having the most wonderful dream. This time, when he slugged the guy who patted his ass at the gaming center, the station security bulls had bought his story of provocation and not thrown him back into lockup for Captain Mam to have to bail him out for the fourth time in one stationside ship visit.

Took three blinks of his still-muddled eyes to connect the klaxon at wake-the-dead volume with what that entailed. Holly the jump pilot/navigator was showing an emergency—an emergency she was breaking protocol by responding to. The jump pilot was not supposed to do ANYTHING before the post-jump handoff to him, except in an extreme emergency. The "oh, shit, we're all gonna die right now" kind of emergency. In-system pilot was a completely different set of reflexes and mindsets, which he had and a jump witch did not. Ben's heart did a dead stop for a second as he contemplated death at 23. Yes, he was Fleet, but dead in a ship was not dead in a VR game. It was for real—the machines don't revive your body when it's dead.

It was an extreme enough emergency that the lunatic jump witch was doing a radical reposition, one that slammed him against his seat restraints faster than he could grope for the emergency shock-me-coherent shot. Idiot Holly hadn't the situational awareness to plot one of these maneuvers, much less execute it. Hadn't a clue as to the ship's red-line parameters. He could visualize frying components and stressed systems.

The shocks of the reposition vectors almost jarred the ampule out of his hand. Skinned his knuckles despite the padding on his jump couch. The vibrations were knocking him back so he could not even get himself to upright position to pilot from. He could smell the fear sweat on her from across the bridge.

However, naked terror can partially override jump trank. Ben's mind was starting to zone in unaided. Whatever the emergency, having Holly the jump witch red-lining the ship past specs on the reposition was waking his mind up fast. He got the shot in with the second try. Missed the best insertion spot and gave himself a hell of a bruise, but he could feel the needle click home. His brain snapped into gear, and into focus. It was like mainlining glacial runoff. Ben lived on his abilities to hyper-focus on positional problems—that's what in-system pilots did. Hours of boredom alternating with moments of action-packed terror. He was both terrified and exhilarated, totally in his element; the pain was happening elsewhere. He wouldn't deal with it until some calmer "later". He pushed aside a fleeting thought of wanting to pound Holly silly. That also was for "later".

He keyed his board to return control of the ship to him...and saw he was frozen out. "Holly, you psycho! Give me control!" He couldn't do his job without a live board and live screens. It jarred him out of hyperfocus, which caused near physical pain.

One frozen instant later, lights flashed and his screen was working. Showed a big hostile, battle debris, and a few plasma clouds that used to be somebody. But he was still locked out of the controls. Holly was emitting sounds, but nothing coherent. Slam! Another reposition by her, dodging potential hostile fire tracks. Fire tracks that she lacked the instincts or reaction time to deal with. Instant terror. Ben screamed...and suddenly his board was green. Someone had taken charge—Ben would deal with who later. His mind was down to lower brain reflex level on anything that did not immediately relate to his pilot function. Hyperfocus. The sounds and smells of the ship vanished from his mind as he became an extension of the machine he was piloting. In-system pilots lived in symbiosis with the ship. Much of what they did bypassed the higher brain functions. You either had the reflexes and situational awareness, or you didn't. Ben did. He simply had no awareness of the rest of the universe when he was in full focus.

Until scan gave him data, he was doing that job as well as pilot. Three repositions later, he had a vector that felt safe enough for him to notice the world again, his brain shifting out of hyperfocus. The hostile did not seem to be repositioning to counter. In fact, it looked...dead? Asleep? Not hostile? What the fuck? Coming down, Ben was suddenly aware of every ache and bruise on his body, of the fear toxins in his blood. He was exhausted and hugely hungry. You normally hit the nutrients straight out of jump to replenish the organic machine that was your body. He could hear noises that were probably words. Perhaps in a few minutes, he would be able to understand them again. Coming down from the focus did not leave an in-system jockey fully functional for a bit.

Someone had either tranked Holly down or knocked her out cold. Her head was lolling and her normally acid tongue was silent. The icon on his board for her chair showed hers in sleep mode. Showed Scan Primary up, with Katanga feeding him possible/probable problems based on guesstimated cloaked hostiles or the big target coming alive. Showed what looked like the remains of two or three corvettes drifting near Randy's Place. Nope, drifting near the *remains* of Randy's Place, a tiny habitat/fueling station orbiting a giant super-Jovian, which in turned circled a dead proto-star six jumps from Nowhere and eighty lights beyond the Edge of the Beyond. A place no one found by accident. Shit!

Chapter 2

Former Master Sergeant Elizabeth Windsor came out of the jump trank fog to an emergency klaxon and a ship doing a violent reposition. For a split second, she thought she was back on her old ship, *Tasmania*. Senses played tricks and she was smelling and hearing the familiar patterns of troop deck in a combat emergency. Then reality overrode memory and she was back on this tiny ship, back to being Fleet instead of Marine. Shit. Life sucked sometimes.

Winnie got slammed into her restraints by the save maneuvers from Ben the Boy Wonder Pilot. Oops. That wasn't Ben. It was Holly the lunatic jump witch. Clueless at in-system and doing it anyway. Shit! She was not surprised at chaos on the bridge. Life had taught her well. Expect the worst and plan accordingly. Officers made the messes and then Rankers cleaned them up. To Winnie, every drop out of jump space was a combat op until proven otherwise. Only way to deal. You came out ready for deployment to combat stations. Little Rimrunner like this shouldn't forget that basic rule of the universe.

She also hit with her "wake the dead" ampule on the first try. She'd taped it into her hand before tranking down for jump. Learned that one from a dead mate back when she was a new meat newbie on *Tasmania's* troop deck. When you signed onto a ship, you knew nothing. You were new meat. Marines didn't bother with training establishments like Fleet Officers did. Troop deck taught its own. She had come on to *Tasmania* as a surly teen brat who only knew the mining ship she'd be born on. She had learned fast. Some didn't. Those mostly died. Marine made sense to her. There was a Marine way of doing things. You learned fast and never bluffed on how much you knew.

She did a quick scan of the rest of the bridge crew. She was the only one fully coherent. Figured. Didn't ask why dealing with pain-in-the-ass Holly was her assignment. Troop deck taught you that one fast. When it all went bad, just deal with it. Command could put her on report later. The shit always flowed down to troop deck and down the chain of command from there. Holly was freaking out. Bad drugs or a real big hostile in system? Deal with that later. Winnie's board was dead anyway. Why? That was Katanga's problem. On her Rimrunner, *Eagle Totem,* she had left IT repair to Amina. On this temp duty, she had done the same with Katanga. She did physical systems and left the software to people who thought in circles. Code monkeys were weird.

Ship was supposed to be at .7 G on the art grav. Something else that was wrong; it was off…or maybe nonfunctional. Winnie could worry about that later, if there was a later. She'd rigged a line to handle free jumps before tranking. SOP. She'd learned that one after her old ship, *Tasmania*—took major fire right out of jump and the art grav cut out without even a warning siren. She had still been partially shiny from new, with a lot still to learn. She'd been left helpless in her hammock while the old hands improvised lines to move everyone to damage control stations. Her corporal had knocked her upside the head to be sure the lesson stuck. Only way a Ranker learned anything. After all, she'd seen the vets doing the line set before trank-down and hadn't asked why or just copied them like a smart Ranker.

As soon as the engines cut out from the second reposition, she'd triggered the fast release on her restraints and leaped across to Holly's chair. She ignored the bitch's incoherent rantings. Let the captain deal with that off the recording system. Fast hold across the fool witch's windpipe, a jab with a trank dose, and a quick flick of her boards to sleep mode. Spared herself a fast glance at the secondary scan screen first. Big hostile. Could be a battlecruiser. Fleet didn't run those in singles or this distant. Fifth Reichers did. Stone pros, those boys, even their nasty genemod killer penguins. She'd lost good mates fighting them. Still, better them than the crazy Hajis. Either variety.

Those thoughts ended as Ben started doing more repositions. Jarred her loose from her hold on Holly's jump couch. Even with her line, it slammed her around the bridge past the other couches until she got a handhold on one of the grab bars near the door to the snack galley. Winnie chuckled. She'd need two teeth regenerated and some bones would need repair shots. Tasted blood and felt pain. Familiar sensations. She wasn't some Navy type to worry about minor stuff. Marines were dead or alive. If alive, you stayed on mission and let the meds deal with what broke. Hell, she'd had a couple limbs blown off when a corridor clearance on a supposedly dead hostile went bad in two frozen blinks. She'd gone from assistant section leader to squad leader in one turn of the fate wheel from that one. Senior surviving. Didn't let them trank her down and get her to the med machines until she'd finished the op. Marines had their rep to uphold.

Pity she was now stuck on this tiny tub and had to pretend to be Navy. Everyone was called an Officer. As if. She was Winnie. In her head, she was a Ranker, a Marine. Someday she'd find her ship again and get her life back. Until then she'd stay on mission. Question was, what was the mission now beyond ship's survival? Meetup with *Eagle Totem* was blown. For all Winnie knew, so was *Eagle Totem.* She'd raise a glass next station liberty to their shades. But no way a Rimrunner fights a battlecruiser. So, time for someone to order Ben to line them up for jump. Time for the Captain to take command. Right on cue, Captain was issuing orders. Officers. They tell you which SOB needs killing.

Chapter 3

Katanga. He was Katanga. Katanga Wa-Benzi. He was scan tech on the Fleet ship, *Nantucket Prime.* He needed to imprint himself on his current identity each time he came out of jump. He never tranked down fully for jump. He was no nightwalker or jump witch who could move and function in the sensory chaos of jump space, but it was the one time he could be himself instead of his current identity. He had had so many identities that the imprint was mandatory. He had mnemonics that triggered the right memories.

Alarm klaxon got his attention. Something major was wrong. He mimed hitting himself with the "wide-awake" shot. Had to stay in character and his current ID supposedly tranked down.

Lunatic Holly was screaming incoherent phrases and doing a radical reposition. His sensitive nose could detect the flop sweat coming off her. Crazy lady was panicking. Also, his board was dead. Or as dead as that technical incompetent jump pilot could make it. Took him all of fifteen seconds to route around her block on his board. Took him 90 seconds more to free the rest. His hands flew over the touch screens faster than even his eyes could follow. Someone had helped her. She lacked the IT skills for what he was maneuvering around. He hadn't thought she could find contacts for malware this good at the bottom-of-the-barrel station they had done repairs at, but someone had sold her this. Or sold her something else that, in fact, did this. Holly lacked the expertise to tell the difference or the judgment to ask him before she meddled.

His attention was on his boards, on the software, so he heard rather than saw Winnie take out Holly. Winnie was hardcore.

Once Ben had control, Katanga concentrated on a scan. Passive only, of course. He was saving active for the first hostile fire track. Why give the techs on the hostile an active to spoof or ride? Strange, he wasn't getting active back. The still-intact hostile showed near to no energy emissions. As if it was dead. The plasma clouds and wrecks didn't add up to enough firepower to give a battlecruiser heartburn, much less cripple it. Opticals were chancy at this range, but the big ship just didn't show enough damage to be this dead. Yet, it was acting dead. Almost as if someone had blown it internally.

By the time Ben had finished repositions, Katanga was setting up possibles/probables for him. Something didn't add, so there could be cloaked ships here. Or cloaked escape capsules from the battlecruiser. Battlecruiser looked Fifth Reich. A *Dachau-*class variant. No way to be sure at this range without actives. The concept that one of those crews could have been infiltrated boggled the mind, but here was the seemingly dead ship, just drifting on a vector that made little sense in terms of system real estate.

Katanga ignored Bridgit screaming at him. Nominally, she was Captain, for as much as Captain meant on a ship this small. Rank mattered when you dealt with outsiders. With a Fleet Ship or a station. Shipboard, everyone had their roles. During combat he sat scan, which made him back-up on weapons. Winnie wasn't at her board, so he was both. Captain Mam could scream all she wanted, but he was keeping weapons live until something about this situation made sense.

Captain kept screaming that he safe his weapons. Katanga shouted back that she should pick a vector and have Ben take them into jump. Better jumping blind than being the next ship fatality in whatever happened here. Screaming stopped. Captain got icy calm. BAD sign. When she did that, it was just before she killed things. Katanga worked his fingers over the touch screen. On her board, it would show the weapons as safed. On his, they showed live. Who did she think did the IT work? Boards showed what he wanted them to. She'd catch him eventually. Might even kill him. It was a chance he was prepared to take.

Chapter 4

Captain Mam, Bridgit Finnmark, was pissed. Not an unusual mood for her, she sardonically admitted to herself. She had been against this whole split of the two-ship working group from the beginning. Yes, *Nantucket Prime* needed major repairs, repairs that few stations this far in the Beyond could do. Still fewer that a Fleet ship could trust to do them. Yes, it made little sense for *Eagle Totem* to be stuck with port leave at that dump. Bridgit didn't care about sense. You didn't split a squadron just because the crew would cause trouble on station. Crew made trouble on station leave. Hell, the two worst problem children, Holly and Ben, had made enough trouble to be a Marine company on their first station leave in a decade. Small ships, small stations, shit happens. Sane people don't sign onto Rimrunners. Sane people who get there by accident find ways to get transferred.

Now *Eagle Totem* appeared lost and she was stuck with this hybrid crew. She chuckled. Not the ones she would have picked, but she had worked with worse. Winnie she respected, if not quite trusted. Winnie had her own agenda. Ben was trainable...to a degree. Katanga she didn't trust as far as she could throw. She did not believe he had truly safed his weapons. He looked too calm. He was a worrier. Good in a scan tech. A lot of scan work required paranoid pessimism. Holly was nuts, even for a jump witch. Bridgit debated just killing the bitch and living with blind jumps until she could pressgang a replacement. The thought made her happy, but she resisted the urge. She had learned to resist her urges as a price of command.

Not that commanding a Rimrunner was exactly like commanding a real ship. It was more a matter of herding cats onboard and acting as a negotiator to the wider universe. Still, it was a position she had worked hard to get way back when. On

Nantucket Prime, she answered to no chain of command. She was as Fleet as she felt like and an independent free-runner when she didn't feel like it. Sort of.

Right now, was one of those sort-ofs. A free-runner would have done what Katanga wished. Blind-jumped toward a known star and risk getting sucked out of jump by some uncharted cosmic garbage. No jump witch meant you took your chances that way. Still better odds than gambling that a seeming-dormant battlecruiser was really dead or that whatever had caused this mayhem had left system. The loot available from salvaging the wrecks wasn't worth the risks of getting real dead without warning.

However, the last repairs had depleted the ship's funds. Fleet Intelligence always bought data. For a detailed after-action report on a battle this size, they would pay big. Big enough to replenish the lost funds and then some. Enough for the upgrades she wanted. Enough to afford a bit more in crew. For lots of stuff. What they would pay for a detailed sweep on a Fifth Reich warship dwarfed the probable price for the battle report. And if her people found working electronics, the price went still higher.

Bridgit felt her mind get icy calm. Told herself that she had already reached the decision she thought she was pondering. "Ben. You're on standby. Oxy mask on. Get that breathing and heart rate under control." She watched to be sure the boy followed orders. Coming out of hyperfocus, he could be oblivious. Winnie disengaged from her perch after Bridgit had gotten the art grav back on. Trailing a bit of blood, Winnie got his board to standby and Ben starting his comedown exercises. Winnie was good troop. Pity the ship had no other Marines for her to run.

Bridgit sent Winnie back to med section to get started on patching herself. Told her to check brig on the way. She got up and walked to Katanga's board. He couldn't hide the screen fast enough. She had him. He faced her with level eyes and a shrug. She backhanded him one and watched as he safed weapons, transferring their control to her board. She then pulled him by an ear to Winnie's board and had him repurpose it for scan instead of weapons.

With weapons and pilot on her board now, Bridgit returned to her couch, now upright in chair function. She could do routine in-system piloting, but preferred to let the computer handle it. She programmed it for least fuel to the battlecruiser with an every-ten-second semi-default to Ben's board. Not that this would save them if that battle cruiser came alive. Nothing would save them from that. Shrug. This was the life she chose and some of the bills were coming due. Better to reign in Hell. She'd done her decades of serving what thought of itself as Heaven. She felt alive, all her senses engaged making her crew perform, making her plan work. For all her bitching, she loved the life she chose. Made her laugh. She caught Katanga working hard at not looking. Such joy to dominate a man that strong....

Chapter 5

Aagney Ruiz had come out of jump sleep just fine. He paid no attention to the radical repositionings. The ship would live or die. Shit he could do about it either way. The mess in his life that had led to his "signing on" to *Nantucket Prime* was years in the past. Now all that was left was fleeing the consequences. He needed this ship to call at a port far enough into the Beyond for him to snag a berth on a ship truly bound so far off the end of the grid that Fleet was a legendary demon instead of an ever-present reality. Until then, being a semi-prisoner on a Rimrunner was as good a case of hiding in plain sight as he could manage.

The Ruiz identity was his last one with any sort of a backup when checked. Someone answering to that name, ID, etc. had once existed on the far edges of Fleet space out beyond Old Earth, further out into the spiral arm. How that person had materialized here, deep coreward into the arm and a good 170 lights beyond the mushy Frontier would be a mystery for Fleet Intelligence to ponder. Hopefully, they would assign a low enough priority, as this ID had already been passed to a light cruiser when the two Rimrunners had done a routine data swap at a dark point.

He put a proper smile on his face when that bitch Winnie came to fetch him. She had just "volunteered" him for a corridor sweep on a supposedly dead Fifth Reich warship. A sweep where she'd be armed and he wouldn't. No use complaining. To the rest of the crew he was expendable meat, and corridor sweeps could turn bloody in a nanosecond. Still, this could be profitable. He hadn't signed on for a full share, but they would throw him something when they cashed in. That hypothetical ship to beyond the Beyond would want payment for his passage.

Chapter 6

Winnie piloted the sled across to the drifting Fifth Reich warship. Captain had given her Ruiz as volunteer labor. Winnie had refused to let him arm himself. Didn't trust him. He got a skin suit. Enough to keep him alive in vacuum. He also got a tool belt, but nothing he could stab through power armor with. She also froze him out of the sled's controls. No way some conscript meat was abandoning her to scurry back to ship. Winnie was in full power rig with weapons, Marine boarding-party style. Dead ships often weren't all the way dead. Clearances could be a stone bear.

Getting the rest of the kit meant bargaining with the captain. Winnie would have taken every mobile droid the ship had. However many you had, you never had enough in a big ship once it all went bad. Captain worried costs and inventory levels. That's what Officers did. Shorted you now so there would be some for later. Sometimes that meant a blood price. Other times it meant a blown mission.

At least this one lacked the biggest traditional risk. Boarding party was always expendable. If it all went in the pot, your ship would run more likely than not. You don't lose everyone trying to save a few. Rumor on *Tasmania* had it that old-timey Earther units would spend blood to recover dead. Winnie filed this under the slag pile of other supposedly old Earther fairy tales. Warrior kings before genemod who mated with bears. Officers who pulled magic swords out of ferroconcrete. Swords made out of pure light wielded by wizard warriors who could project themselves backward and forward in time. Yeah. Sure. Just like the tales of streets paved with gold bricks and Blue Skyers who rode atmosphere down gravity wells by flapping their arms. Winnie wasn't even sure Old Earth was a real planet. The idea of everybody once living on some rock was absurd. Besides, rocks were settled from orbit, not the other way around.

Anyway, this time there was no way for the ship to flee. A Rimrunner was too small to run from a Battlecruiser at ranges this close. If it was all a trap, everybody died, probably all at once. Winnie mentally shrugged. Marines didn't die of old age. They died on mission or they died helpless in their racks on a ship-to-ship fight. Winnie had always hoped it would be on mission.

Enough thinking. The docking port was in sight. Everyone rigged theirs slightly differently, but form, to some extent, followed function. Winnie had seen enough types where she was sure she could puzzle this one out. She got it open in under 20 standard Terran minutes, then popped a small, flying droid through to scout inside. It's how Marines did it when there was time and this was a no hurry op per the Captain. Officers set those mission parameters and Rankers like Winnie made it happen.

Chapter 7

Holly Kim had returned to consciousness securely belted into her pilot's couch. She had a sore windpipe from where Winnie had choked her and a raging sort of hangover. A normal crewman tranked through jump space. The trank and jump between them took their body down to a near state of hibernation. Way low metabolism, no excretion, and near-catatonic stillness. They came out kilograms lighter with a massive hunger for both calories and nutrients. Witches force-fed before jump where possible. Shots of vitamins and key nutrients, plus a large meal heavy on protein and sugars. Only a rare handful could manage eating or indeed ingesting in any form in the physiological chaos of jump space. Coordinating sensory input and limited bodily motion was tricky enough.

Someone had doped either her pre-jump shots or the heavy gluttonous meal. Probably the same someone had put the malware into the IT systems. Holly often picked up weird shit on stations to try out for the next jump. Keeping the body working in jump space was an art not a science. No one really understood how the drive worked or why her body functioned in jump. She'd found out she was a witch on her first voyage all the way back when. Even with trank she hadn't stayed fully under. That ship's witch caught it and talked her through the terrors, through the chaotic jumble of sensory inputs.

He'd also introduced her to sex in the chaos. After that, sex in normal space just felt wrong. As if she were half alive and her partner was a meat robot. Great. She was stuck with the kink on a one-witch ship. Nothing she'd ever volunteer for, but Fleet was like that. "Impressment" they called it. Kidnapping is what it was. She'd only heard of Fleet in horror stories before that encounter. She was from so far out that Fleet was as much a myth as both the supposed homes of humans, Terra, and Tau Ceti. As if. Humans came out of the galactic core. Everyone knew that.

The hangover was from whatever had doped her. She had a real problem. She was missing the last two days on station and everything that happened afterward until she woke up to be cursed out by Captain Bridgit. As blank as if someone had put her under the hood and done a peel-and-scrape. Which was flat-out impossible. The ship had the equipment, but the Captain wouldn't use it on her and then not tell her later. Bridgit was a stone bitch, but not petty that way.

So, someone was seriously fucking with her. Question was both who and why? Katanga was the obvious answer, but Holly had learned to distrust easy solutions to shipboard conspiracies. The politics of a small ship could be convoluted. For now, she was content to watch the boarding action unfold. She hoped she wouldn't be sent over. Stripping dead ships could be tricky and sometimes fatal. Most ships had boobytraps. Yet, if the Captain had her pegged as being trouble, then Captain Mam wouldn't trust her on *Nantucket Prime* where she could slip off with the ship to elsewhere, leaving the away party stranded. No, indeed. Shit.

Chapter 8

Ben watched the screens from the two drones doing recon on the battlecruiser's hull. He had flight control, but left it to the autopilot. Similarly, the expert system screened the video and IR feeds automatically, but Ben wanted to devote himself 100% to observing. He knew the limits of automatics and experts. He trusted his mark-one eyeball over anything that could be programmed. He knew ships and what could go wrong on a granular level. He'd leave all the theory for weirdos like Katanga. He'd been pushing cargo off stations since before he'd turned twelve and doing in-system piloting before fourteen. He'd seen damage in all its many forms. Meteor strikes, internal explosions, sabotage demo-charges on hulls, company police missile and beam strikes against independents. He'd seen it all and done a fair bit in the other direction.

The nowhere system he was from was a constant simmering pot of petty corporate despotism mixed with endless minor rebellions. He'd been ever so glad when *Nantucket Prime* had dropped into his system at a time when he was stationside on a mechanical for his mining ship. He'd been at the docking gangway when Captain Mam debarked. Had asked about signing on before she even dealt with the customs or dockmaster's office. Once she'd said yes, he sold his ship share fast and was camped out ready to depart long before *Nantucket Prime* went up on the boards as listed for departure. Rumor said Fleet ships paid no attention to rules, left when they felt like it. He'd later learned this was often true. At the time, all he wanted was off, was out. He'd never regretted it for a moment.

For once, he and the expert software agreed. The big ship had been blown from the inside. Sabotage on a massive scale and multiple locations. This was bad and good. Meant the ship probably was dead, which meant it wasn't going to come alive and kill him. Ben understood dead. So dead even the machines can't rebuild you. Machines that only the richest of the rich could afford where he came from. Machines he was now entitled to by right as Fleet crew. The bad was that whoever or whatever blew this ship could still be alive somewhere in the wreck. Alive and waiting to be taken aboard to kill him, to kill his ship. So, he watched and brooded.

Chapter 9

Ruiz worked his way through the airless corridors, brushing aside the dead bodies. There were both Aryan "humans" and their genemod killer penguin companions. So far, most seemed to have died from decompression. It appeared as if someone or something had vented the air and cut off life-support backups. However, there were scattered places where the same creature or creatures had used explosives. Or triggered embedded boobytrap explosives. Supposedly, Fifth Reich ships were impossible to infiltrate. Supposedly.

Things were different out here in the Black. Ruiz had come out of a Fleet birth lab and then a Fleet creche. He and his mates had been hatched as Fleet personnel, based on some procurement algorithms that were way above his pay grade. Most hatchlings, as they called themselves, never questioned why they were Fleet, any more than a fish in a tank questions why it swims in water. Ruiz had always been different. He'd worked hard to hide it and been partially successful. He'd also broken away from the career tracks. Most stayed in the interior Fleet directly garrisoning Federation and adjacent Fleet Space. They were hatched, educated, trained, and served in peace...most of the time. There were occasional rebellions or Wrecker raids, but even on a combat ship inside the Frontier one could go decades without ever firing a weapon except in sims.

The glory hounds opted for combat ships that went beyond the Fringe into the Diaspora. They saw themselves as real warriors instead of time-servers. Ruiz chose the Beyond, but put in for administrative training. Admin, finance, personnel, procurement... they had no glory, no status. The trans-Frontier commands were a maze of semi-independent warlords in practice,; however, Fleet they all were in theory. He'd played the game. Played it too well, in some senses. He'd made enemies, but he'd also learned things—built up a modest nest egg if he could somehow arrange passage to where he'd parked it. Which seemed unlikely right at the moment.

Right now, he'd settle for getting his three missing fingers back. Not all the traps had been triggered before they had arrived. He'd triggered two so far. Two die rolls with real forever-type death. He'd been lucky to have only lost digits. Fingers just meant time in the med machine attaching the new ones after getting them printed. His skin suit was smart fabric. Did an automatic seal around the punctures. This feature could be overloaded and had definite limits. Tighter limits than the smart armor of a Marine power suit, and he'd bet Winnie had modified her suit to be even more protective. She was obsessive on her kit and gear.

These Toymakers were tricky. Reichers created weird tech. That's what gave them the "Toymaker" nickname. Weird, over-engineered equipment, often past the cutting edge of even their tech base, much less Fleet's more restricted knowledge of the sciences. Federation had been technophobic back to Old Earth. Something about the color green and some New Age, whatever that was. Fifth Reich ships usually self-destructed to avoid capture. Now he was part of a crew that had a mostly intact one to study and strip. Captain Mam wouldn't give him a full crew share, but even a partial would be more than his own nest egg and much easier to access. A new thought hovered at the edge of his consciousness. Corridor crawls were often fatal, and a few less members of the crew meant more to share around for the survivors. He kept trying to repress the thought for fear he would follow through on it...and get caught trying. But it would solve SO many problems.

Chapter 10

Winnie was using her IR screen face-plate setting for the corridor crawl. Dead ships vented to space weren't quite deep Black space-cold. There were a few degrees' difference, which mattered to tech-services types for calibrations. Shrug. To Marines, they were cold enough where ANY live power showed as a heat source, even a well-insulated or masked one. Power could be equipment, life support, people, weapons. It could be a lot of things, but what it wasn't was dead stuff with no juice. Dead stuff cooled down until it was ambient, which in this case was well down toward 120 degrees Kelvin, whoever he was.

Winnie was getting heat. A few live connections. Wisps of heat trails from distant sources. More than could be accounted for by being star-side of the wreck. More than could be accounted for by cooling from alive days ago. She been trailing a big one through decks. Had lost two droids to traps. Might have lost a few more or maybe they were in electronic dead spaces and couldn't report in. Corridor crawls on ships and stations were old hat to Winnie. It's what her kind of Marines did.

Winnie abstractly knew there were Marines who did drops onto Blue Sky worlds, mostly from the battalions and regiments in the big ships in the pacifier squadrons. She'd partied stationside with a few of those a couple or three times, but it wasn't her scene. Why drop onto a world? Just come out of jump at high fractions of C vectors and hit the damned rock with inerts. Coming in fast enough, you didn't need fancy warheads or maneuver. Techs had some big equations for why it worked. Two old-timey guys named Newton and Einstein had invented the weapon. Winnie didn't care who two -centuries-dead tech services clods were. It was a big hammer and the rock was the nail. She'd seen it done to stations, to asteroid bases, to mining setups on airless rocks. After the inert, there was still the corridor crawl to make sure. Bridge Officers decided when you did what. To them, Winnie and her fellow Rankers were just meat weapons. So what? To Winnie, Bridge Officers were meat machines that generated missions. Way of the worlds. Marines did missions and she was Marine.

Winnie had been trailing cable back to the original docking port. Only way to be sure of communications back to Captain Mam. Now she stopped and requested backup. Taking a live compartment was more than a one-person job. Too much could go wrong too fast without backup. She asked for Ben and Katanga. Ben was reticent about his former life, but he'd let enough slip. He'd done some serious fighting before. Not just ship-to-ship across the Black. Up close and personal. Besides she liked his reaction time. She asked for Katanga because while she didn't trust him or Kim, she had nothing against the witch and hated the IT guy. His superior air bugged her. He'd make a good piece of expendable meat as point dog through the door into whatever. If she got him wasted, she could rig her board for scan and weapons until Captain Mam got another warm body. She wished she had her own IT tech, Amina, instead of this asswipe. Amina was a born liar on her past life, but did acceptable work as far as Winnie was concerned. Winnie doubted Amina would have had an info system an idiot jump witch could have fucked over.

Ship had other power armor rigs for them. Not as good as hers. Regulation Marine suits. Winnie had "improved" hers. Real Marines always did. The suit kept a Ranker alive or enough parts of a Ranker alive to get back to the machines for a rebuild. Winnie knew Rankers who'd lost every piece over time. Even a brain could be printed and rebooted. You lost whatever memories you had since the last download. The joke was that this was mission amnesia. The hardcore types downloaded mission data from other sources and simply took a guess on where/when/how they had gotten their heads blown off. Fleet was conservative on new tech.

The Hybrid Crew

Took forever to get it made official. Winnie spent a lot of her pay on upgrades, tweaks, add-ons. There was always new stuff out there. Captain Mam wouldn't give her ship's funds, so the other suits stayed standard. That was the tough luck of whoever got to wear them.

She'd asked for Ben and Katanga. She got Katanga and Kim. Winnie magnetized her boots and took a break to wait for them to catch up. Time for her to earn her pay.

Chapter 11

Holly Kim cursed herself hoarse suiting up. No one else cared or even listened. So what? It was her way of blowing off steam. Captain Bridgit was making a point on how pissed she was. Ship normally didn't risk a witch doing an away-fight. Witch was too mission-critical. Captain was labeling her expendable. Means she was really willing to risk blind jumps. They weren't safe, but what really was in the Deep Dark? Worst part was Holly didn't blame the Captain. She had a memory blank. The malware probably had come from her. Only she couldn't explain because she didn't have true memories to lie from.

Her suit was Marine standard. Not what she was used to, but she coped. Her weapons were her own mix. Off her old ship, *Curse of Mordor*, she'd done away-work when needed. Who got sent was a mix of rotation, favor points, and the fluctuating politics of a small ship that traded or raided as opportunity took it. Winnie went for what passed to a Marine as cutting-edge tech. Holly went with what she had experience on. Sometimes it was centuries behind Marine issue. Other things were not so much better as just brut different. When it dropped in the pot, you relied on reflexes. Holly used what had kept her alive before. Corridors and compartments were tricky spaces. Many ships had oddball internal designs that had just evolved over time. Many shipyards out in the Deep Beyond, out past the supposed end of the Diaspora, had hull templates they'd been using back to when they were grey or black colonies in Terra's Outer System, before the Diaspora had even reached the twin planet once known as Pluto.

One thing gave her comfort. Captain might hate her, but Winnie didn't. No love between them, but not the cutting hard dislike she always had from Ben and Katanga. Let Katanga be first through the door. That was the suicide posting. Kim even stopped cursing on the scooter ride across. She wanted to seem less a bitch to Winnie, to cement that Katanga was the most expendable.

Chapter 12

Katanga Wa-Benzi used a standard-issue suit and just grabbed the first weapons and tools packs available. No way he was giving the others a clue into his past, either real or the one the Wa-Benzi ID had, by showing preferences. He wasn't a boarding-party type, but he could handle himself well enough, or so he thought. Combat got his full reflex package and discovery be damned. He'd laid enough contradictory trails on who or what he was to this crew where he could pass off anything by just refusing to engage when they questioned him. They would argue their absurd theories with each other, laying a distortion shield on the realities. Which was all he needed anyway.

He laughed to himself that he was so deep into this character that he was even thinking in Lish. Lish, in some of its many forms, was as close to human standard speech as there was, even if it were not the language he had been born with. He doubted there was anyone who spoke THAT within a hundred lights. As is, he was fluent in Lish, even multiple dialects thereof. Crew spoke the most common dialect, Mercan. Captain Mam clearly was fluent in Beeb as well. He'd seen her use it talking to senior Officers when they met big ships out in the Dark. Higher Fleet Officers out here in the Beyond regarded Beeb as their tongue and looked down on the lesser breeds who only spoke Mercan or, even worse, Val. Kantanga could pass for a native speaker in all three, as well as half a dozen others.

He'd stayed quiet on the scooter, ignoring Kim's endless patter. He didn't argue when Winnie shoved him on point. He'd expected it and besides, she ran away-parties. She had the training, the former rank, and the Captain's backing. No use fighting gravity or inertia. The way to minimize the loss on some conflicts was refusal to engage. He spotted the heat trail she had been tracking. It led him down ramps, ladders, and corridors, followed by more ladders to a deep interior compartment in what he guessed was engineering country on this ship. Winnie wasn't allowing time for careful inspection but what he could see had that look. Even with Toymakers, function somewhat dictated form.

The compartment showed as sealed. His instruments seemed to indicate atmosphere and life support on the other side. Winnie positioned herself 15 meters back on one side of the door. She sent Kim 15 meters beyond. Ruiz was behind Winnie with the remains of his hands manacled. Katanga laughed to himself. Winnie was taking no chances with that wild card of a man.

Katanga was going to be tasked with breach and entry. No surprise. The surprise came when he began to attach his breaching charge. Ruiz gave a scream over the intercom and jumped away to avoid a rapidly descending door that had suddenly materialized. Winnie easily clubbed Ruiz down and shouted a "Hold!" command. Another barrier had appeared on the far side of Kim. They were trapped, at least for the moment, by barriers they hadn't seen before they had clicked into place. Suit showed atmosphere rabidly filling the sealed space. Instrumentation said breathable, within Terran norms, and no visible chem or bio surprises. Suits could be spoofed. Before any of the three intruders could dream up a new plan, the compartment door popped open swinging into the compartment, not out at them, on hinges not visible from the outside.

Before Katanga could react, a voice sang out. It sounded human and somewhat girlish. "We surrender."

Cutting over it was another voice, louder, but having some trouble formulating the words. Didn't sound fully human. "Don't believe a word she says!"

Chapter 13

Winnie still sent Katanga in first. When he didn't get fired on, she advanced to the doorway herself, prepared to cover the room with her slug thrower. What she saw inside amazed her, and Winnie prided herself on not shocking easily. Inside was a live Elite SS Killer Penguin. It was two meters of genemod on a penguin frame. Winnie didn't know exactly what penguins were, but it had short legs and pseudo-simian arms with digits attached at the end. Other than the pads on the sort-of hands, it was covered in soft, short, white and black feathers. Supposedly, the twin coloration was that of an Earth Reich superwarrior species, the SS. The beak was not really suitable for human speech, which probably accounted for the slightly garbled sounds it emitted trying to speak Mercan. Winnie had thought the Reichers had their own language. Chermin? Doysh? Winnie hadn't really paid attention to the lecture, and never bothered with the imprint. They never let themselves be taken alive, so why care what drivel they spoke? She just carried suit implants for machine translation on some thousands of languages and dialects, including the Reichers', Woggish, and even Beeb in the rare case a higher naval Officer noticed a Ranker existed.

This one had what looked like steel manacles imprisoning its legs. The leg irons in turn were welded to the compartment's wall. He'd then been covered in a semi-sticky shock net. Only his head was free. He (it was quite obvious the creature was male) had harnesses for tools and weapons (all empty), but no clothes per se. The head was frantically turning back and forth between Katanga, Winnie, and the room's other occupant. She was another genemod, a BarBee. Basic structure was human female. She was 165 centimeters tall with measurements of 100 at the bust, 35 at the waist, and 90 at the hips. The legs were impossibly long and the straight corn silk-blond hair ran down past her ass. The sky-blue eyes were somewhat overlarge for the otherwise too-perfect face, making her appear a tad childlike. Winnie had heard of them, but had never seen one. The Reichers hatched them. Fleet's techs swore the combination of measurements were impossible, but the Reichers lived up to their Toymaker reputation with these.

BarBees were the most renowned organic sex toys in human space. The little female was worth a fortune. The often-technophobic ragheads prized them, called them whories or something like that. Both types of Woglah-loving Hajis also used genemod sheep for such needs in their all-male crews. The BarBee had her tiny hands wrapped around one of the largest shock pistols Winnie had ever seen. She made eye contact with Winnie, somehow instantly guessing who was in charge, and slowly lowered the weapon. She blew Winnie a kiss and smiled. She was very softly singing some song about a girl named Alice. Winnie was sure it was centuries old, and even more sure she'd remember it eventually. Someone on *Tasmania* had liked this music. It was a tip-of-the-tongue, sort-of almost-memory. Winnie put that aside. She had a room to police up.

The black-and-white bird was squawking not to believe the BarBee. He was claiming he was Fleet Security. He was offering up recognition phrases. Winnie knew them all and some went back over a century to her certain knowledge. Winnie took imprint tape for that sort of data. What he didn't have was anything less than two decades old. Which made it all suspect. "Got anything current?"

"I've been under longer than you've been alive! Get me out of this. Grab that little monster before she bewitches you."

Winnie outright laughed at him. Fleet Security running undercover was weird enough. Fleet Security this far out beyond the Fringe was weirder still. The two together was near-preposterous, not counting how the Hell he'd gotten imprinted into one of these sort of bird-things and gotten a serious warship to take him as crew. There were stations far enough out in the Deep Dark where Fifth Reich warships could dock, or so troop-deck rumor ran. Troop-deck rumor also often denied that the Fleet had a Board of Admiralty or even that Federation was real. Few Rankers came from the tame, civilized interiors. Still fewer knew shit about a wider world than their ship, the stations they docked at, and the other ships whose people they partied with or feuded against as times changed. *Tasmania* had a multigeneration feud with *Arctic*. One set of rumors said it was over some operation that had screwed the pooch, with each Captain blaming the other. Another set of rumors made it the result of a drunken tryst between the two captains on some station circling a nameless dark point, where Captain Mam of *Arctic* had laughed at Captain Sir of *Tasmania's* tiny organ and lack of stamina. Didn't matter why. New meat learned which ships were friends, which were foes. The "why" could be left for senior Officers and inveterate barracks tale-spinners. "Give me one reason to believe you?"

Before he could answer, the BarBee did. "He can't. He got bad tape and thinks he's Fleet. I kept him alive for questioning, hoping a Fleet ship would show up." The BarBee paused and then sang rather than spoke the next part, "Go ask Alice."

Winnie prided herself on a good poker face. She wasn't a card sharp, but she could handle herself at a poker table. You played anything and everything in a ship's company. So much dead time between missions. Now she wished she had set her face shield to mirrored, to not show her expressions. That phrase at that pitch was Fleet Intelligence. It was one of the deep-set recognition cues. Winnie had taken tape at this clearance level when she'd made Sergeant. Fleet Intelligence DID operate out in the Deep Black, beyond any vestiges of where Fleet even patrolled. Security covered what was known. Intelligence chased what wasn't known. The two squabbled at the interface. Intelligence used cover organizations, ran multigeneration penetrations. Supposedly, they had links to real aliens. Not some slug or fern from a blue-sky rock.

The Hybrid Crew

Fly their own ships and enough weapons to fire back, even on a pacifier squadron of battleships aliens. Supposedly. Still, the deep-set signals could be compromised. Anything could be.

The BarBee couldn't see her face clearly and nothing should be able to read her mind. "Don't trust me. No need. Just stick us in different brigs and have your Captain find a level-three or higher Fleet base. Their databases will know the truth or enough of it. By the way, I'm Buffy." The pseudo-fem smiled at Winnie and blew her another kiss.

The SS Penguin went berserk at this. "Kill us both, if you have to, but don't let this demon spawn onto your ship! Don't trust a word she says. She's Haji, not Reicher. She'll blow your ship like she blew this one. She'll trick you like she tricked me."

Buffy smiled. It didn't fit the semi-juvenile features. The face looked early teens, even if the body looked clearly adult. The look was no longer innocent; it was feral with overtones of mocking. "I'll take the test. Print up pork and wine. I'll ingest both. Scan me before you move me to your ship. No hidden bombs, no weird devices. Just a functional brain, which is more than birdman here has."

The penguin went berserk at that. His ranting got ever less intelligible until they were mere squawks. He was spraying a fine cloud of spittle to go with the noises. Winnie mentally bagged both of their claims. She put her mind to figuring out how to find them suits so she could vent this section again and get back into comm with Captain Mam. Let the Officer sort this one out.

Chapter 14

Holly Kim had been left guarding the two official prisoners, as well as the de facto prisoner, Aagney Ruiz, while Katanga and Winnie exited to try and work out the controls for the blocking doors that had sealed in this section of corridor. Holly found this amusing. She regarded the Marine as a functional idiot. They had their way of doing things and were simply blind to the wider universe. Marines didn't take prisoners often in boarding operations. So, they didn't carry the kit to deal with prisoners. Hence the search for "suits".

Holly had no doubt the Reicher ship had dozens of penguin-sized suits for the big bird. She'd already seen dozens of dead penguins and hadn't seen that much of the ship. Whoever had vented the atmosphere and killed life support had achieved surprise. She hadn't seen anything sized for the BarBee, but... fitting small people into large suits was no big. It was the reverse that got tricky, although much less so if you didn't care about the prisoner's pain and discomfort.

Holly had never cared before. Her ship's people were not pirates, at least not full-time. They were opportunistic. They would raid or trade or whatever seemed promising. Their loyalty was to each other and to their sort-of clan of interrelated ships. They had stations they called on where they made sure to be on best behavior, but that was prudence. Station security knew them for who and what they were. You came in under the guns of station defense batteries following very tightly ordered vectors. Deviation was met by hostile fire. Trust was not part of the equation. You made dock, fenced your loot or made your trades. You were allowed liberty in a carefully policed set of bars and attached rent-a-rooms. The station bulls patrolled in squads and were hair-trigger attack dogs.

The Hybrid Crew

So, when you took captives, no one cared about damaging them. You stuffed them in anything handy, then decided later whether to kill them, ransom them, or just dump them on a station. You used suits when you had to, but rescue balls by preference. Holly always carried a few in her equip pack when she was doing a corridor crawl. You stuffed the captive into the ball, let it fill with atmosphere and sealed it from the outside. Then you voided the corridor or section. If they punctured the ball, they died. If not, you just attached a tether and had a droid drag them out.

The little BarBee went into her ball with no complaints. She knew the drill, apparently. She was humming some ancient classic Earther tune, or at least that's what it sounded like to Holly. Holly had no taste for most human music. It just seemed like loud noise to her. She was into some sounds she'd bought on a station they sometimes partied at. It was a mix of two Far Diaspora traditions, Gregory's chants and windy chimes. The good new tunes came from way far out Beyond. The BarBee was naked, but Holly patted her down anyway. Checked all three likely hiding places. They were empty, but it paid to play safe. Hajis would put explosives inside and then detonate.

That left the damned birdman. He was jabbering a kilometer a second. Threats, promises, warnings about the BarBee. He was offering bribes, immunities, treasures on this ship. Maybe he was Fleet Security. Maybe he had bad tape and thought he was. Holly really didn't care. What she cared about was how to get the manacles off without letting him get at her. She thought on it for a couple of minutes while the torrent of words flowed onward. The solution she came up with was imperfect, but she had long ago learned not to worry about perfect. She backed up to the door. Handed Ruiz her laser cutting tool after popping the manacles off his wrists. Told him to cut the bird's manacles. First, she set the tool to its lowest power setting. Tested it by burning Aagney's injured hand. Took off a thumb before his skin suit sealed itself around the breach. He'd need to get the hand fixed in the machines anyway. So what? Conscript meat learned about pain. Way of the world.

Aagney got the manacles off. She then tossed him a roll of duck tape. Had him tape the beak shut. Shut real tight. Holly had always wondered why it was called "duck tape". She'd eaten duck out of the printers. Tasted a bit greasier than chicken. She had tried to eat tape once and it tasted nothing like the print. Besides, the tape didn't print on the organic setting anyway. Not even semi-organic. The penguin didn't want to go into the ball. Was hopping and trying to get words out of the sealed beak. She took the cutter back from Ruiz and burned one of the webbed feet. The penguin hopped into the ball and she sealed it behind him. It was a tight fit. He had to fold himself over a bit as he was two meters tall, beyond the ball's specs. Tough. She wondered what penguin tasted like. Decided she'd print herself up some for dinner. There had to be a penguin setting and probably some recipes in the kitchen memory storage. It certainly had enough of them for duck, although so far she hadn't found one for duck tape.

Chapter 15

Aagney Ruiz was in a controlled panic. Fleet Security was not something he was prepared to face, less so on a higher-rated base where the files were more up-to-date. Once they put the hood on him and peeled his brain, he was dead, dead, dead. Why couldn't it have been Fleet Intelligence? Intelligence would have sold him immunity for what he could spill. He had enough dirt on finance and admin personnel to give them ammo in dozens of the endless intraservice food fights they and Security reveled in. They'd get the core stories from the peel, but he had backup data-cubes stashed on a station along his travel route. He'd spent good money on a twenty-year dead storage locker. Uncommon even for Deep Spacers, but not so absurdly so that the service wasn't available. Intelligence could give him a new identity. Could...but would they? That was always the question. They normally paid for good info. Said it encouraged folks to find them, sell them more. Didn't mean they couldn't just peel him dry and then pop him out an airlock. Or sell him back to his former command. That could be a cold, slow, painful way to die. He had burned those bridges behind him. Not that he'd had much choice but still....

The BarBee would be no help. She clearly had her own agenda. When asked for the key to the bird's manacles, she replied with a sarcastic laugh and a scornful expression. Both of which looked strange on those ever-too-sweet features. The bird's babblings might be more useful. Aagney was prepared to discount half of what he spouted, maybe more. But he'd blurted the outlines of how to work the corridor doors. He had offered locations that held spendable treasures, not just intel data that needed a Fleet base to which to sell it. He'd even claimed there was a functional jump-capable courier ship in the main hangar bay. Functional might or might not mean functional right now as opposed to after a month's maintenance, but right now Aagney didn't feel he had a whole lot to lose.

Holly was focused on getting the penguin, who claimed his name was Fritz, into the ball. While she fried a flipper foot to "encourage" him, Aagney backed out of the room into the corridor. Katanga and Winnie were at the door leading back to the docking bay. Neither was paying him any mind. Katanga wouldn't and Winnie probably thought she'd tasked Holly to watching him. As if that witch took direction from anyone except her Captain. She'd been impossible even with Captain Mam, to the point where Aagney had expected Bridgit to just burn the witch down and live without one for a bit.

One foot at a time, Aagney slithered to the far door, the one that led deeper into the ship. It was now or never. The controls were right where Fritz said they would be. Aagney worked them fast then rolled under the door as it started to rise. The second he was through he hit the control on the far side, slamming it closed. Just in time. Winnie got three slugs under the door in the seconds it took to return to its blocking position. Ruiz lost two toes, which threw his balance off. He compensated and ran. Ahead was a ladder, just where the idiot bird said it would be. Aagney swarmed up it faster than he thought himself capable. He was free! Now to find the courier boat and then see about one of the treasure lockers.

Chapter 16

Winnie wasn't stupid enough to keep sending slugs at an armored door. She was proud her three-burst had made it into the rapidly dwindling space before the door sealed. Her suit had add-ons that improved her aim way beyond what Marine suit basic gave you, but then what was a Ranker to spend pay on beyond partying and gear? Small-ship duty didn't give you a gang of mates to party with, and this two-ship unit didn't do all that many station visits beyond resupply and repairs anyway. So, Winnie geared up. No Marine Officers here or even senior noncoms to question her choices. Plus, she'd always been a gearhead. She wasn't sure she'd hit the bitch-bastard, but she liked her odds and didn't like his. He was already short fingers. If she'd taken out a foot, he'd be slowed but good. She doubted he could get Reicher med machines to work for him...but he'd gotten the door to work first try. A door that she and Katanga between them still hadn't puzzled out.

That logic train led to Holly and the two prisoners. One or both must have spilled while Winnie was trying to work the door. Holly denied everything. Denied, but wouldn't let Winnie do playback on her suits vid and audio pickups. Pulled rank, claiming only Captain Mam had the authority. Winnie was tempted to just waste the fool. She had the authority. Shipboard ops were her thing. She doubted Captain Mam would approve. Could be one of the two prisoners was the info source. The sex toy or the bird with the taped beak? And they were both inside rescue balls and thus safe at the moment from physical "persuasion". How convenient for their supposed guard. Winnie was definitely asking Captain Mam to let her buy some new meat. She wanted someone she could train to watch her back. Having a clone of herself would be tricky but they could tag the newbie with purple hair or something. Buy a grown piece of meat, tape herself over, and then

she'd have someone who wasn't both clueless and so damned
sure of themselves that they wouldn't take direction.

Chapter 17

Fritz was past both panic and anger. What he mostly felt was pain. The Fleet bitch had burned the webbing on his left flipper badly with the laser. It would need hours in the machine. Except Fleet machines weren't set up for penguin. So, either he somehow got one of these vermin to let him get treated shipboard before the transfer to their craft, or he would be left with a very generalized healing shot that sort-of might work on anything that was mostly Earth-stock DNA. Which he sort-of was, but "might work" was not a pleasant thought. There were so many painful ways this could go wrong. Yes, it could also kill him, but it was pain he was keen on avoiding. Death just meant the pain stopped. This damned mission had been a rolling disaster. He'd be dead, but a new version of him would be hatched who wouldn't have any memories of the last thirty or so miserable years.

He was surprised which of his two captors had taken the bait he had held out. It wasn't that anything he said was precisely a lie. He'd just left key pieces out. Things that could save him and perhaps doom them as well. It all depended what the fool tried and in what order, plus how badly Buffy had sabotaged his ship. Buffy. She'd been Brunhild when she'd tricked him. When the courier had brought her in, the manifest had listed her as Bibi. That damned trickster witch probably had forty more names where those came from. The tech specs on BarBees said they had minimal intelligence. Just enough brains to follow commands and read moods. The "read moods" part was accurate. She could read body language to the point where he'd sometimes thought she was telepathic. She could also fake empathy. Or turn it on and off like a tunnel diode. She'd played him. She'd played them all. She'd crippled this ship and he hadn't a clue as to why. There was no way she could have known there was a Fleet ship coming or even that it would find their compartment while doing a search. He couldn't even make sense of why she'd kept him alive. He was breathing air she would eventually have needed. Or was she really a witch and had precog? Prior to knowing her, Fritz had been a most convinced materialist. Now he was beginning to think at least some of the supernatural rumors about witches and demons might be true. He couldn't find a material rational way to explain her. Damn her.

Chapter 18

Katanga used the distraction and Winnie's absence to open the supposedly locked door. He'd known how to do that before he set foot on this ship. His problem was that he didn't care to explain how he knew. None of the tissue of lies he had woven for these two crews about the Katanga Wa-Benzi identity allowed for a person who knew Reicher tech, much less their ship schematics. Instead, he had been playing along with Winnie's fumblings while trying to ascertain how on Earth the sensors had been rigged to seal this corridor section and restart life support and atmosphere. Someone had done some really elegant patches. He had theories of how it could be rigged, but wasn't sure how accurate they were. All should have set off screaming warnings from the maintenance semi-autonomous systems any large ship had. Someone who could write a hack that could subvert core systems to that degree was worth study and careful evaluation. He might be in the presence of someone beyond his own capacities, and he'd never seen anyone on his level since leaving home.

He had a decision he was hoping to avoid making. He lusted after access to the programming cores to get the details to the hack. He equally feared letting such powerful code loose on his own ship before he had mastered it. This left the problem of explaining all this to Captain Mam without her twigging to how much he wasn't telling her. He'd signed up for Fleet to make a journey. A journey he couldn't make on a commercial ship. Merchant ships did not traverse the inner spaces that was Federation. They took you to stations where you were screened for entry to Federation Space. Katanga thought he could fool those machines, but he wasn't sure. Failure was not an option. If detected, they would know that his people still existed.

Fleet's history of the Exodus from Earth was badly corrupted.

They had re-edited it so often that entire centuries had disappeared down the memory hole. Old pre-space Earth was centuries further back than the current official histories allowed for. Entire anti-Wrecker campaigns had been expunged. Elements within Fleet had less-corrupted histories. There were security programs still there to flag his kind. A kind that one set of records denied ever existed and another somewhat deeper set asserted had been firmly and finally exterminated. Reality was otherwise. Remnants existed, had been chased further into the Diaspora than even Fleet patrolled. He was both a messenger and the message. He had to find his way around the slowly expanding cloud that was Federation Space to near the other side before heading further out to where another remnant of his people was supposed to be. Communication this way was ultraslow and chancy. More direct means risked discovery.

All of this was a background monologue in his head as he went through the now-opened door and reconnected to the comm cable to speak to Captain Mam. Cable back to the docking port. Tight beam laser across to the ship. Captain Mam was pissed at the comm blackout. It wasn't his fault, but he was the one there to feel her wrath. She had a temper. He let the anger flow over him, was properly professional and deferential. In under two minutes, the tantrum had passed. Captain Mam had clear orders. Forget the missing fool, Ruiz. Everyone else back to the docking port. She would come across with Ben and take command.

Chapter 19

Captain Mam Bridgit Finnmark was both elated and pissed as she suited up. The pissed part was easy. Winnie aside, her crew had proven near-useless in a simple operation. Regardless of how much she would set aside as ship's operating funds, their personal shares would leave them quite wealthy. Enough to buy their way off the ship, if that was their fancy. More than enough for whatever luxuries they lusted after. Even the naturally obtuse Holly Kim should have been able to figure this much out. Between what they would strip from the ship and the two prisoners, this was a huge payday. The captives themselves would fetch top prices. Both services paid well for recovery of their own and paid even more for delivery of folks falsely claiming to be members. A small part of her wondered if she could start a bidding war, as each service would want both of them.

The elated side was the too-good-to-be-true opportunity. A Reicher major ship killed by sabotage with its data and equipment all intact. Normally, you took a hulk after extensive battle damage plus last-minute scorched earth by the defeated crew. Bridgit distrusted luck this good. Someone had done this. One of her prisoners? Both? A third party? Life had made her a pessimist with a quite jaundiced view of human nature and luck. The Sainted Murphey was an optimist in her view. Which is why she had arranged a small ship command for herself. It limited the risks and maximized her personal control of situations.

Right now, the situation she wanted control on was greed. It was bound to occur to her crew that fewer survivors meant a larger payday. More so if one of them got control of *Nantucket Prime* and just left. Blind jumps were risky, but not insanely so. Ditto for running the ship with a crew of one. A sole survivor could invent any fantasy story for Fleet when the sale was made.

Faced with a windfall this big, no Fleet base commander would waste time with awkward questions. The regular Fleet regarded Rimrunners as little better than licensed pirates anyway. They would short the survivor on price. That was a given, but even half-price on something this big was a vast fortune for a lone operator, not even including the resale value of the ship.

So, she needed to rig the ship to make this impossible. She'd put the best blocks she could on the IT, but had no doubts Katanga had installed backdoors. She could set the ship to suicide via scuttling charges, but that was a bigger risk than she was willing to take. Katanga might still be able to work around the commands and might trigger the charges by a botched bypass attempt. So, it was complex manual lockouts to the rest of the ship from hangar bay. To those she added various concealed explosive traps and anything else that could make stealing the ship difficult. She'd had such preparations ready for years, but was smart enough to realize that Winnie and probably Ben could puzzle their way through, given time. Her final line of defense was to send Ben through the open hanger door on one scooter; then, after he was halfway across, exit with another, pausing to voice-lock the mechanism to her suit. She had left large ship command to reign in Hell. Time to make her demons work in-harness.

Chapter 20

Ben Redson was content to let Captain Mam set the defenses excluding him. She took care of command paranoia so he didn't need any. It was funny in its way. He was the only member of his crew who actually wanted to be where he was, doing what he was. Winnie wanted back to the big ships, preferably her old berth on *Tasmania.* Holly would desert in a flash if there was a chance of going home. She might anyway just to be someplace less structured. The demons of the Deep Dark knew what Ruiz or Katanga wanted. In neither case was it spending the rest of existence on a small ship cruising the backwaters of the galaxy.

Ben had never considered enlisting in Fleet. The few ships that called in his system were patrol corvettes. It seemed like working for one of the big corps. The corvettes had a circuit of a dozen or so systems they patrolled on a regularly fixed schedule. He'd gamed against guys from them on station, had shared pitchers of beer. It was all rules, fixed watches, petty discipline. He could sign onto a Merchanter and do the same. Ben didn't do well with rules, structure, authority figures. That's why he'd been an independent from the time he dumped school and started pushing cargo. He had the reflexes. He was a quick learner. He also had an affinity for machines.

He'd got his real start as a gofer in the maintenance bays. Knew a guy who had a cousin who knew a shift boss. The pay was minimal and off the books. Credit in a shop in the in-systemer section of the station he'd been born on. The friend had shown him how to trade the credits for cash to mining ship operators. One slot had led to another. Pusher, fixer, asteroid miner, atmosphere scoop driver...one time or another he had pretty much done it all. Independents shifted positions to the slots the corps didn't monopolize. Given a choice, the corps would do everything and freeze the indies out. Problem was, they were never very good at what they did. Too many bosses who didn't know shit and refused to learn. They needed twelve levels of meetings to decide anything. The Suits who made the decisions knew nothing beyond "management science", whatever the fuck that was. So, they'd make a mess, and then contract out to the indies to fix it. Then try to push the indies back out once the mess stabilized.

Corps also couldn't cooperate for beans with each other. They would form a united front against the indies on something like claim-jumping, then backstab each other doing under-the-table deals for heavy metals or rare earths or whatever the long-haul Merchanters were paying top credit for this month. The corps were big fish in his system, but were below insects even on a Sector level, much less in the real Fleet Space economy.

Made for an endless low-level struggle between the indies and the corps, plus the indies had their clans and rivalries. Ben had seen action, but it was sporadic and very low-level. Ships got mines attached to them. Parts got "improved". Company claim beacons got "lost". It was an endless low-stakes negative-sum game. Ben didn't design games, but he was an avid player. This was the sort of world he hated gaming in. The rules were set to slow decay of everything. That was his star system. Decade by decade, things got a bit worse for everyone as more and more effort was lost in the endless petty warfare.

Ben had heard of Rimrunners. They were glamorous. They went where they wanted when they chose. They were a road out of the box he'd been born in. A road whose start he had no way of finding...and then *Nantucket Prime* posted on the in-coming boards. New ship names posting was unusual. New ship names with a Fleet designator were unicorn-rare. Luck had been with Ben. He'd been on station when *Nantucket Prime* came calling. He didn't know it was a Rimrunner. He only knew he had to take the chance. He knew a girl who worked comm for the Dockmaster's office. He'd hovered at the right spot to catch her coming off shift. His looks had worked for him. They often did in life. Being good-looking was a blessing and a curse. She'd accepted the drink invitation. She had other things in mind, but he kept her drinking and talking until he got the data nugget out of her. Two Rimrunners in system, with one doing a station call. She got what she wanted. He even paid for the hot-sheet room. Usually with his looks, he paid for neither room nor drinks. It was worth it. He got a time, a docking slot, and a Captain's name. He was there waiting when Captain Mam made dock and came down the tube to station.

Everything he owned was in his duffle at his feet. He'd imagined he would have to plead. She just looked him over, laughed, and asked what his skills were. Then cut him off partway and said he'd have to take a peel. When he didn't back off, she gave him a time to report in. He'd spent those two days saying his goodbyes. There hadn't been many. He'd had a lot of acquaintances, but damned few friends, and still fewer among the living.

Which was why Captain's setting the defenses on him was so funny. What the fuck would he do with a huge mound of money anyway? Buy his own ship? Spend his time being a commander dealing with crew, with Fleet, with the universe? As if. He never wanted to be in charge of anything. Captain was a good boss by Ben's standards. She let him do his thing with piloting and machine maintenance. She never asked him for social skills he didn't have. She bailed him out of station brigs and never slapped him around too badly for it. Give him that pile of credits and sure he'd buy a hotter ship with better acceleration. Then give it to her and sign to serve there. One of these days one of their cruises would kill him for real, never-to-be-resurrected dead. He could have saved himself enough by now to pay for resurrection insurance, to have himself rebooted. Not for Ben. That would be a bad copy, not him. Until he got wasted, this was the only life he wanted. He was exactly where he was supposed to be in the universe. Captain Mam chose the destination. Some witch dropped you in system and then it was on him. Life was just a better VR game with weirdo scenarios anyway.

Chapter 21

Holly Kim was considering possibilities as Winnie formed the group into a column to troop back to docking and link up with the Captain. Katanga and Winnie were in the corridor while the bird had done his babbling act. Ruiz had made his move while Holly herself was weighing the odds. She knew her rep for not looking before she leapt. True enough in small things, especially if she were bored on some nowhere station. The rest was a cultivated front. She preferred being known as an impulsive maniac, to being judged inferior, just because she liked knowing her odds and wanted to puzzle out the smart move. The universe just didn't always make sense. You needed an angle, an edge. And while she was figuring hers, the bland nothing that was Ruiz had made a play. A play that fixated Winnie's eyes on her. Shit!

The Captain would pull the vid and audio off her suit by a simple radio command. Captain had the rank priority built into her power suit. Holly could try to destroy her suit's memory with the damning data from the bird. That would save her for maybe three minutes until the Captain slit the tape on the bird's beak. He'd babble it all given a chance. No, if she was going to use this opportunity to get free, it had to be before link-up with Ben and the Captain. She had no doubt she could kill Katanga before he knew what hit him. She was equally sure there was no chance of surprising Winnie and less than no chance of a quick shot penetrating her suit. Winnie had layered all sorts of extra features on her suit. Holly had not paid attention to the details. Normally Winnie berthed on *Eagle Totem*, but the two crews had done liberty on enough stations to gossip. The gearheads would talk equipment. Holly would ditch them all, find some more interesting company. There was no way to truly make a suit totally immune to hand weapons, but Winnie would have the latest, cutting-edge add-ons. Besides, on mission she always seemed to have extra senses and eyes in the back of her head. The suits allowed 360-viewing. Normal people like Holly couldn't really cope mentally with more than 180-degrees, but Winnie seemed to live in the 360 with zero seconds of delay on processing.

The bird had been clear about a courier ship in the hangar bay. That ship, plus a sled's worth of the usual precious metals, and she could find her way home. She'd find a good dark point and wait. There were often Merchanters looking to do off-the-books deals at maybe twenty she could think of. They all had multiple IFFs. Fleet made folks use them by simply regarding any ship without one as a target. However, smart people had extras, so they could switch identities at need. No way to know the one she would buy wasn't on some watch list or other, but as long as she wasn't broadcasting a Reicher IFF there were enough shady stations and shadier fuel ports to keep her ship and herself alive until she could remake contact. Best bet would probably be the old Prescott Habitat. If none of her clan's ships were there, the supply house they fenced their loot through would probably have a lead. She'd best take the bird along, in case the courier or the hangar was password-protected or something similar. Birdman had made it all sound too simple. Life never was. For now, all Holly could do was dog it on the movement. She kept falling behind, claiming she'd seen something important worth bringing to the Captain. This ship was full of Toymaker tech. It was such an easy lie.

Chapter 22

Katanga Wa-Benzi led the column. He did not deliberately lag like that idiot Holly the witch. She had data he lacked. Something the bird had told her. It was obviously not the doll. The bird's gaze was fixated on her while the BarBee was tracking all her surroundings.

Holly would try to escape. Let her go. One less opponent. The key was getting access to the data cores. For a prize this great, he would risk breaking cover. A hack this spectacular was a weapon almost beyond price. His people needed this. Needed it far more than the message he bore, the message he was the meat representation of. If necessary, he would share the outlines with Captain Mam. She would be satisfied with the concept, whereas to him the key was the code. He wasn't even more than marginally aware of the corridors he was walking down, of the ladders and ramps that led from deck level to deck level. He was thinking of how he'd have broken the code, of what to look for. He had the ability to put his body on what amounted to autopilot while his mind worked a problem.

Chapter 23

Ben was at the dock awaiting both Captain Mam and Winnie's inbound party. He was using the time to take the lock's controls apart. Winnie's party had been trapped by descending doorways that functioned also as blast doors. Ben wanted to be sure a similar unexpected freezeout didn't trap them all on the wreck. He'd seen too many abandoned mine claims with similar traps for the unwary. He really didn't understand the whole Fourth Reich, Fifth Reich, Wrecker conundrum. The higher politics of the Diaspora were Captain's Mam's worry, not his. She set the course. He drove the ship and worked with gear. This was a whole new set of gear to learn, to master. Weird, but not too weird. They used metric measurements, not those inch things or some of the even more peculiar ones he'd seen since he joined up with Fleet.

Chapter 24

Fritz was terrified. If the fool he sent off on a treasure hunt didn't do something quickly, he was getting dragged back to some backwater base where he'd be years proving his credentials. All for a blown mission courtesy of that little liter-sized blonde bitch. He couldn't decide which was scarier, that she was Fleet Intelligence or wasn't. Either way, she was pure poison.

Chapter 25

Winnie didn't quite have eyes in the back of her head. She didn't need them to know Holly was mentally fitting her for a casket. She could read body language, even through a suit. A standard-issue suit whose weak points Winnie could hit first shot every time. She halted the march and turned on Holly, clearly aiming her slug thrower. Told the bitch to either make her move or take point with the bird. Ignored the backtalk and kept her weapon leveled. She was settling this now. No idiot without Marine rank was going to give her this much shit and get away with it.

Chapter 26

Aagney Ruiz had navigated several levels and a lot of ship interior corridors to reach this hangar bay. He was not sure if it was a hangar bay or the, as in the only, one. Didn't matter. That courier ship was right in the cradle where the bird Fritz said it would be. So far, every access code the penguin had blurted out had been valid. Now all Aagney needed was for the codes to get the courier ready for launch to work. The main hatch was open and the command bridge was easy to find. There were too many couches by Fleet logic, but the command chair was obvious. It was massively larger. The system boot-up was easy. It needed a password, but it took the one he had. It took a few minutes to puzzle out which touch icon was maintenance. A prompt came up over the screen. A command authorization request. The bird had given him the answer. Aagney entered HIWI as instructed...and everything went wrong. The hatch sealed. He could see flashing lights. He was getting screen demands for prompts he didn't have. OH, SHIT! The bird had tricked him.

Chapter 27

Captain Mam was coming across when she saw signs of life in the ship. Navigation lights were coming on. Ship seemed to be powering up. Shit, shit, shit! All her people were inside. She had no way out. She kept the scooter on course, cursing her luck. So close to a huge windfall and now THIS!

Chapter 28

The blast seals slamming down on this new section of corridor clearly disconcerted Holly. Winnie was not distracted. The target remaining Holly. She was peripherally aware of atmo coming in. Sound was starting to happen, as well as flashing strobe lights. Not the cues Winnie was used to, but the message was obvious. Someone had triggered the expert systems and the Reicher ship was going to general quarters. That was for later. The Holly issue was now. She kept her slug thrower on target. Holly panicked, lowered her weapon, and turned on the penguin screaming curses. The bird was agitated. The BarBee looked exasperated. Winnie ordered Katanga to open the rescue ball and let the BarBee out.

Chapter 29

Katanga let the BarBee out of the rescue ball per Winnie's orders. Buffy darted forward as soon as released, opening an access panel that was in no way visible to his quite careful gaze. She had made a noise to cause this to happen. It was not language as he understood such things. It sounded like a mating call of some mud ball's wild beast. Katanga enjoyed watching nature videos about mud balls. He was not interested in actually going down a gravity well, but found the idea that creatures could live in them strangely absorbing.

Her hands flew over a recessed screen. She was inputting data, augmenting or commenting on this with a stream of words. They sounded like language, so he presumed words. His suit was programmed for over ten thousand languages and dialects, but was only picking up stray words. Either the mix was a code or what she was saying was older and more obscure than even he could imagine. It came out as "Garble garble noise helper squawk grunt garble noise noise coiuratonis noise noise penguin garble squawk override 6gh87vy izdaga gesag", or something like that. The machine translation was in a pitch that alerted him that the expert program was guessing and had alternate possibilities available if he wished them. On reflex he told it to save those. That was for later. The atmo was up to life-sustaining, but the lights and sound had stopped.

"I killed the effects here, but can't reverse the security alert without getting us to the data center. Fritz here gave your deserter a code that amounts to 'intruder alert'. What do you want? To regain control of the ship or escape? Not sure I can do either, but cannot do both at once." The BarBee finished her speech with a truly exasperated look, which looked almost silly on her overly pretty features. Apparently, the seeming teen sex doll was nowhere near that naïve on the inside.

What Katanga wanted was access to the data center, but without company. He had long ago learned that what he wanted and what the universe offered were not the same. "Winnie. I'll take the chance and accompany her to main data. I'm the only one with the skills, so why up the risk? The rest of you work your way to docking and link up with Captain Mam."

Chapter 30

Holly Kim was enraged. At the idiot bird for a treachery that looked likely to kill himself along with Holly and her shipmates. At Winnie for being a hard-ass Marine who was fixing to kill her. That Winnie would win the gun fight, Holly had no doubt of. Marines were scary. They looked human but acted like descendants of the legendary Terminator superwarriors of Old Earth. Holly had courage enough. Her clans killed their cowards young. Called it "culling". Bad individuals were poor breeding stock and unworthy shipmates. Marines had iron discipline as well as bravery. Set a Marine on a mission and they followed it to the bloody end. Shit! Her clans were warriors, not mission-oriented legionaries. If something looked too expensive, you broke off and cut your losses. It was save the ship and then, if possible, save yourself. Knowing when to go 'no mas' and break it off was what separated the clans that lived from the ones that died in the Deep Dark. A ship would never make next rendezvous and folks would wonder for a while and then forget them. It was their way. It was the way the universe should be.

She eased her hands away from her weapons and did what Winnie wanted. Took point with the bird in its rescue ball. The small hairs on her spine stood up as she did so. She was less than certain Winnie wouldn't burn her down anyway. Holly simply couldn't follow Marine logic. How could you be loyal to people you didn't know or to missions that served people you'd never meet?

Chapter 31

Ben Redson had disabled the defenses on the locks before
the lights began to flash. General quarters was a military thing, so
he thought of it in terms of the emergency warning lights of his
misspent youth. The comp and the expert programs screaming
that you were screwing the pooch were old friends of Ben's. He'd
lived by knowing to a nanometer how far over the limits he could
push some piece of equipment. He could barely read now and was
near-totally illiterate when he began his career as a runner on the
in-systemer docks servicing the miner ships. You learned by doing
with visual instruction tapes as supplements when he been shown
those existed. You learned what to do. More important, when
to do. Why it worked was something he learned much later as a
confirmed gearhead. All the little luxuries his Fleet existence gave
him now were absent during his wasted childhood. His star system
was poor by galactic standards. The corps hogged what cream
there was and the scum-sucking Corp Rat Suits with "management
science" degrees hogged most of that.

He hadn't learned the big words until he'd been Fleet
for a while, but it was a giant, negative-sum feedback loop.
Everyone cheated at the margins for crumbs while the system
slowly decayed. So, you learned to work in near to no light, in
uncertain gravity, with jury-rigged parts. For Ben, rejiggering
this lock was easy. He had amazing lighting. He had a suit that
was a tech marvel. He may have been working on a Reicher
lock, something he'd never seen before whose specs he could
only guess at. However, each part was high-grade milspec with
triple redundancies. That was how military did things. They had
resources. They had suppliers who actually produced to spec
some of the time.

His suit had record functions so he could call back what

the lock had looked like at each stage of disassembly. His meat memory was good. His suit's expert systems were near-perfect. Ben knew he could have taken tape to upgrade his meat brain. Winnie did these all the time. Ben was afraid to let anyone mess with his mind. Milspec tape still meant trusting a supplier, trusting the supposed good intentions of a chain of command. Ben had been bred to a far more pessimistic view of the universe. He laughed to himself. Labeling himself as a worse pessimist than Winnie was scary, looked at objectively. So not worse. Different. Winnie simply accepted different risks to stay on mission. She lived for missions. Ben just wanted to stay alive and keep flying the ship.

If the battlecruiser was semi-alive again, it would send droids to repair the damage, to expel the intruder. Droids were a luxury beyond what his star system afforded people. Even the corps only had simple centuries-out-of-date ones. Even the few Fleet corvettes that called seemed not to have current ones. Ben had partied with some of their gearheads, talking equipment between rounds of VR gaming and beer. The real Fleet had cutting-edge tech, almost as good as what drifted in from the Far Beyond. Reicher supposedly were the actual best there was. Best, but finicky. Toymakers. One-of-a-kind designs often little better than prototypes.

So, Ben rigged a trap. A few simple sensors and a voltage arc to fry what came. Two droids got fried in rapid succession while Ben planted himself on the hull outside the docking port. He gave it three minutes, but no third appeared. Told him the ship's defense programs only rated him an annoyance. Which was just the way he liked things. He radioed Captain Mam and told her he was about to start dismantling the fried droids to save them. She ordered him to hold back until she arrived. She was four minutes out. Ben shrugged. He was content to let someone competent make these decisions. He'd rather be back on his ship, anyway.

Chapter 32

Captain Mam Bridgit Finnmark had spent the scooter journey over weighing her options. She could grab her pilot, cut and run. On one level, it was the smart move. Pressgang a new witch and run short-handed until funds improved. A bit of creative semi-piracy would probably see to the funds. However, it would take time and, in the interval, leave her with a barely working ship. It also meant admitting defeat, something she knew she was not good at.

She thought of trying to actually take control of the battlecruiser and return to Fleet with it as a prize. The potential payout was tempting. The risks were insane. It meant trusting Katanga and her prisoners. She didn't trust any of them. Had both ships been here and both crews been available, it might have been possible. Maybe. Barely. If everything worked just right. She filed this in her head under "maybe later". Recruit a second ship or, still better, two more, and return. If the Reicher battlecruiser was still there, try to steal it. Even split with three ship-shares and twenty crew-shares, it was the payout of a lifetime. Bigger than finding a full working copy of some new version of *the Prophet's Last Wife*. Any version was an insane lure to ragheads and thus worth a fortune to Fleet Intelligence. She'd never understood the Woglah worshippers. It was just a kiddie-porn snuff entertainment and not an especially good one, although the anime versions sometimes weren't half bad. Dirty old men and little girls with dolls? Boring.

That left some version of get the prisoners and some electronics out. She could count on Winnie to head for dock. Winnie followed orders if possible and had the brains to divert if she felt the odds sucked too badly. Ruiz was no loss. She doubted he could run a ship this big on his own. Whether he starved or the security bots killed him interested her not in the least. So, the big decision was whether she held the dock or tried to link up with Winnie. Logic said hold in place. Bridgit was not the passive type. She had Ben trigger the next door in. Using the magnetic setting on their boots, they fought their way through the gale of exiting atmo, then closed off the door behind them. Ben claimed he had the door on manual. Bridgit was sure he thought he did, which was as good as it was going to get. Onward they went, following Winnie's comm wire.

Chapter 33

They were four corridor compartments closer to the exit, to Captain Mam, to some version of safety, when the spiders began dropping from the ceiling. It was ultraspooky, as if the ship was making up its mind on whether it was still alive. Life support seemed on, but it was spotty. Enough atmo to hear but not well. The art grav had been flickering on and off. So had the lighting. They probably came from maintenance access panels and pathways, but definitely from above. One-meter bodies, eight legs, and what appeared to be organometallic hybrid composition. Also nasty claws, small lasers, and the ability to spit some highly corrosive acid.

It took Winnie fractions of a second to register them as a threat and switch from slug thrower to the hand flamer with which she always outfitted her suit. She had been focused on the flickering changes in ship function and it had slowed her reaction time. Had she still been on HER ship, she'd have gotten her ass chewed badly in the after-action meeting. Marines were supposed to adapt and overcome. If you want it easy, transfer to a patrol vessel and be a pussy with a fixed schedule and nothing more to do than inspections on scared Merchies.

She had the flamer preset to max. Dangerous in close quarters if you didn't know what you were about. Winnie was a trained Marine, not some new meat. She'd seen this vid before. Marines in clearance actions lived and died by fire. You flamed and took flame, fired slugs and took incoming rounds. Flame was a near-universal weapon for corridors. It wouldn't ricochet, it didn't go through partitions and it didn't harm full power suits. At least full suits of Marine grade armor, much less the better composites Winnie wore. She'd flamed humans, machines, and things the after-action report denied existed. One-meter tall synth-life spiders were a new target, but they were targets. Let a damned Officer decide how to write them up afterward. Above her paygrade and glad of it. Winnie lived for combat. It would kill her one day. No one lived forever. Pity she wouldn't get listed on *Tasmania's* wall of honor, wouldn't be part of the remembrance on Camerone Day. They always read the whole list for that one. That the dead should never die.

Holly panicked right out of her head, firing wildly with her laser cutter in all directions, screaming, "Get these suckers OFF me!" Katanga didn't panic. He was using a long, exotic, metal multitool as a club and batting the pests. The bird cowered in his bubble, then howled in pain as one spit of acid penetrated the sphere and scorched his already-wounded flipper foot. He was howling commands in Cherman, probably trying to prove he was a friendly. It wasn't working. The BarBee showed off her athleticism. She was bouncing off walls in a series of leaps and tumbles. She'd swiped a flamer, probably from the highly distracted Holly, and was racking up kills.

A pseudo-spider affixed itself to Winnie's face plate. The plate went opaque, probably from acid attack. Winnie used the flamer as a club. It failed to pry the synthobeast off. Winnie hooked a thumb under it and—upping her strength setting to max—squeezed until she broke it in two. The leaking fluids were burning away outer layers of her suit sleeve, leaving a foaming residue. Winnie flamed it fast. Fire worked on most things. Her suit registered a breeze. Meant the partitions were up, the compartments unsealed. Which meant something bigger was coming. This was bad.

Chapter 34

The last of the spiders were down. Dead? Were they ever "alive" in any real sense? Did it matter?

Katanga had a choice to make and was out of time to weigh options. He could blow his cover or blow his chance at this code. This amazing code. Put that way, the choice answered itself. "Winnie, something big and bad is coming. I'm the only one with a chance of putting the ship's defense systems back to sleep. I'll go. Just don't backshoot me as I leave."

Not even waiting for a reply, he turned on Holly and smacked her upside the head with his tool. It didn't damage the suit's helmet or her head inside. It got her attention, however. Fast. "Enough of your shit, bitch. You run those downloads NOW or we kill you. Winnie can cut your legs off with the laser cutter she's carrying. Smart suit only covers so far. Me, I'll just keep bashing so the smart materials cannot flow as fast to cover your legs."

Holly flared. Screamed curses and threats. Then psychically collapsed and did the inevitable. She activated the audio/visual recordings her suit had made of the killer penguin's initial torrent of words. Dumped it to Winnie and Katanga's suits. Katanga had his mnemonic functions on hyperfocus. He would remember every word, every gesture the damned bird made. It was less than a perfect data library. It would have to do. No time to waste interrogating the perhaps-insane penguin. It was gesturing wildly in the partly collapsed ball. Katanga considered, weighed, and discarded the idea of taking it along. It took him under two seconds and he did not slow down while he did the calculation. He knew where the main data center would be. It was a two-bis variant on the *Dachau*-class. He knew the initial system admin codes and doubted they had ever been updated. He moved rapidly down a side corridor and then up a walkway to the next deck up. There were walkways for high traffic as well as ladders. He knew the schematics as well as if he'd personally prepped this ship in the yards. The braindead Reichers were dabblers in physical tech, but quite conservative in design modules and not very interested in software or wetware. Idiots!

Chapter 35

Aagney Ruiz started to come out Sleepland. The security droid that had popped the courier ship's hatch had fried him with a shock bolt. Now he was in a regeneration tank. Okay. Reichers were sort-of human so they should be able to fix his hands. Be nice to have his missing digits back. He was still coming fully awake when the tank popped open and a security droid retrieved him by using its massive claw to remove him. Aagney tried to stand and…and screamed and kept screaming. He had no feet, no ankles, no legs below the knee. Instead, his "knees" connected to what seemed to be organometallic platforms that he was probably expected to stand on. He went to cover his face with his hands, only they were no longer his hands. Each was massively larger, with two thumbs standing at the opposite ends of five thin, flexible digits.

The droid did not react well to his screams. It lightly shocked him. Point taken. Aagney got quiet. He could hear his heart madly racing and was fighting total terror. He kept repeating in his mind "stay calm" while his breath spasmed and drool ran down his chin. He wanted to say this was a nightmare. He wanted it to be a nightmare. He was all too aware that it was real.

The droid hauled him into a huge compartment labeled HIWI. HIWI. The code the bird gave him. The compartment was full of human, part-human, semi-human, and mostly primate remains. It had been vented badly and maybe hit by explosives as well. There were puddles of blood and what looked like machine fluids. It smelled like something out of the pre-space Hell fantasies. The droid dumped him on a bench. A second smaller droid came over. It had a dozen different arm attachments, each with different tools, pseudo-hands, claws, or devices. It beeped at him in a machine language. Ruiz didn't know how to respond. It tried something guttural. Probably Cherman. Ruiz's suit was gone and, with it, the language implants. Machines don't shrug, but Aagney was sure the response seemed to be something on that order. It pinned his head in place and beeped at a third droid, who advanced on him with a huge needle full of something. A needle that it slid beyond his eyeball to directly hit his frontal lobes. Needles! No one used tech that old for uploads. Only these droids did. And…and Aganey's brain stopped for almost a minute as it integrated the new data and skills. He answered with the proper sequence of beeps and clicks, none designed for a human mouth, but no one any longer cared what he was designed for. He was now a HIWI, a "volunteer" helper. An organic slave…or mostly organic. He knew his task. The droids started bringing him bodies and he started slicing them into useful parts, with the rest put aside as food for him. Orders were orders.

Chapter 36

She could hear it advancing. It clanked. It also hissed like an antique tea kettle. Whatever it was, it was honking big and coming right for them. Holly Kim wasn't into suicide stands. That was for idiot Marines. Fuck Fleet, fuck Winnie, just plain fuck it all! She'd been buffaloed over the playback. Now she had a second chance. A chance not to die. A ghost of a chance to get home or at least close to home and rich enough to buy into a clan ship. You knew the damned bird was lying on some it, but that meant some of it might be true. Worst case, she died later.

Grabbing the tether on the deflated ball the bird was writhing in, she ran down a side corridor. The Killer Penguin bounced behind her, secured to her suit by a come-along tether. Holly Kim tensed, waiting for the shots in her back. Instead, she picked up Winnie chuckling on the suit radio. "Run, you gutless Beyonder Witch! Don't need your yellow ass. And take Fritzie Boy with you. Fuck him blind for all I care. I'll pass along your resignation to Captain Mam." Winnie started bellowing some song. Something about facing a Sun. Her language implants pegged it as some old Earther tongue. The floating icon in her visual field said "Latin derivative", whatever Latin was. She didn't stop running for minutes. As she got winded, she just kept upping the oxy content of her suit atmo, kept feeding herself stim pills. Whatever the big bad had been was behind her, but the terrors remained.

Chapter 37

Winnie was prepared to die. She was fighting for the wrong ship, but the mission was in a right place. Better dying killing the Reichers than doing a bit of approved piracy. Marines did both, but real Marines from big ships like *Tasmania* didn't usually get wasted fighting down the corridors of some one-cannon-carrying Merchie. They fought real enemies—Reichers, Hajis, Independents, even deserters. This was a mission worthy of being on the wall of glory, even if it would never be posted. The thought gave her comfort. She decided to go to her end in proper style. It wouldn't do to sing *Tasmania*'s battle songs. She was not on a mission from **her** ship. She was *Tasmania* from the day she'd come aboard as fourteen-year-old new meat and would be 'til the day she died. But after one classified mission at a location scrubbed from her memory, her mates and those from the other ship involved in the final fight, *Castile*, had partied themselves hoarse at the refueling depot they'd been given R+R on. It took a while for such a two-pump station to refill two sets of massive tanks, even with every skimmer the damned station had working 25/7. They'd learned each other's battle songs.

So, she started belting out songs about facing the sun and old blue shirts. She'd never bothered learning the Old Earth fairy tale history they were based on. At even decades removed, Winnie found the excuses for all wars bleed together. Wars didn't need excuses to Winnie. Humans fought. Always had. Always would. Descended from killer apes or something like that. Another lecture she'd slept through, another set of bullshit she'd been uploaded and had filed under "who the fuck cares?" You fought because Officers told you to. You stopped because the hostiles were all dead or the damned Officers changed their tiny minds again. That's why it was easier up against Reichers and Hajis. They were the perpetual enemy. You fought them because they were trying to kill you. Always had. Always would. Even senior Officers couldn't get something that simple wrong.

Winnie was sort of aware that Captain Mam had once been such an Officer. Big ship, big command chair, staff of dozens. Had chosen small ship service. Captain Mam was vague as all Hell on details, but Winnie had seen big ship Officers pull themselves to attention and salute when Captain Mam had sauntered past in some base corridor. Even people with stars on their shoulder boards, gods that walked. If she ever got back to *Tasmania*, she'd have to ask. She knew enough people with real access to personnel records. Big ships carried the full Navy list. Some entries would be decades out of date but machine memory is cheap. Even if Captain Mam had changed her name when she switched to Rimrunners, there would be the notation of "also see file XYZ".

Only Intel and Security scrubbed their entries on that level. Meant she'd never learn what grade of Officer the BarBee was. Winnie pegged Buffy for Officer. She couldn't place the memory of how she knew, but was sure that recognition code was Officer level. Senior NCOs got so much shit uploaded that you quickly learned how to half-forget what seemed unimportant. The ones that didn't went nuts. Could recall every detail of prebattle uploads from decades past, but could never find the shower in the morning. First round was a good mind scrub under the hood. Second was post them someplace non-sensitive, usually in some low-level base facility. Like that idiot refueling station where she'd learned *Castile's* songs and fantasies of their glorious past. She'd seen dead people with more brain function than some of them. Far better to die in battle. Fleet medcare could keep the sort of zombies alive for centuries.

Winnie could hear the noise getting closer. Clanking, wheezing. Fighting in atmo had its uses. Sound helped. She noticed the BarBee had swiped a pistol and two grenades off Winnie's suit. Winnie never ignored anyone touching her kit, but somehow Buffy could go blank on her. Must be an Officer thing. Maybe the naked sex doll could really fight. They'd see in a minute or so.

Chapter 37

Ben stepped over the still-smoldering remains of the droid Captain Mam had just fried. The corridor was clear again. The droids kept coming and the two of them kept killing them. Grenades, slug throwers, lasers, flamers. One time, Captain Mam had used a metal multitool she carried to beat the meat part of a hybrid droid into blood paste. Whatever expert system was running the defense was dumb or severely compromised.

Ben needed his suit systems to keep track of where in the battlecruiser they were. The corridors had no decoration. Ben had seen functionalist approaches to ship's décor before, but on a ship this big it was, in his eyes, absurd. Everyone he knew added some touch of color, some wisecrack nameplate…something….

Ben wasn't used to fighting any sort of expert systems. Even when you did a raid in his home system and stumbled into automated defenses, it was all homebrew. In his years on the Fleet ship, he hadn't done much corridor-fighting. When it happened, it was usually Winnie and whoever. He and Jennifer, *Eagle Totem's* jump witch, were rated essential personnel. Not this time. The target was too big. Maybe it was too big for one little crew to cope with? The thought scared Ben. He had wanted out of his insignificant star system. He'd been abstractly aware that the vast, wider human sectors of the galaxy included huge ships. He'd never seen a hostile one before, much less from the inside. This was so not fun.

Ben knew he wasn't a coward. He'd been proving that since before his balls dropped, running errands for the gangs that owned the in-systemer docks on his old station. He'd been sent outside to push cargo the first time with a fast, three-minute verbal set of half-assed instructions. He'd managed his sled well enough that no one realized he was winging it. Gang needed cargo shifted fast for some reason. No one ever told the kids why. It was all "hurry up and do it now!" Shrug. Captain Mam wanted this. Making the ship work, finances and Fleet connection, was her job. He'd fight his share until he died. He laughed to himself. Even if he knew then everything he knew now, he'd still have been at that gangway tube asking for a berth. Rimrunner service had proven to be nothing he'd imagined. That just proved how pathetic his knowledge of the Dark had been. His star system didn't rate as a pimple on the galaxy's ass. Out here in the Black, he was alive. He went endless new places. His little ship was part of Fleet, the demon lords of all creation.

He'd been abstractly hearing a set of noises. They made no sense, so he'd been filtering it out. Too many feet, all out of sequence with each other, and the sound slowly getting closer. Now he saw why. Coming around a corner, two intersections ahead, was a segmented nightmare. Each section was a meter-and-a-half high, two meters long, and a meter wide. They were connected by some sort of semi-organic smart material that sort of looked like rubber or plastic. Each section had two or three legs on each side, but none of them matched. Human, simian, animal, mech, and weird combos. There were one or two arms on each side—again near-random in form—but all carrying hand weapons or tools. From the front and top were stalks of what seemed to be eyes, although for all Ben knew they were ears or noses or electromag sensors or...the thing kept lurching forward with more and more sections spilling slowly into the corridor. The weapons were firing at Captain Mam. What demented Toymaker logic was behind this abortion of a battle-bot? What worse horrors remained? A part of Ben's conscious mind was reduced to gibbering, but his return fire never faltered as he kept hammering the thing with slugs. It probably wasn't really alive, so he couldn't kill it. He'd settle for damaging it at the moment. SHIT!

Chapter 38

Buffy's command rang out before the target turned the corner into view. It must have been in a tone that registered to Winnie as Officer's command voice, because Winnie fired before she saw anything fully. Fired at the weak points of a target type she'd never seen before. Buffy had called out what Winnie thought was a string of gibberish before the "fire" command. The weird noises turned out to be a Fleet descriptor code. Marines keep extra data in their suit's memory suite. Memory was cheap and small. Monkey brains in a Ranker could get clogged with too much stray shit, so the vast bulk went into suit memory. Winnie kept a shaved patch on her skull that she slicked well with contact foam for direct access.

The suit memory called up the visuals, targeting, and such. Winnie giggled as she burned the semi-dead construct down. The data came from a three-ship engagement some two centuries back. *Castile*, *Arctic*, and *Kongo*. Two ships *Tasmania* had links to. Felt home-ish. These assembled bits of meat, semi-living parts, and metal were powered by some antique thing called "steam". Big boiler in where the intestines used to be and semi-plastic tubes carrying the superheated water vapor to the limbs. The former brain was a quasi-electric construct, but didn't quite fully control the limbs. Hence the lurching and staggering. Winnie's suit provided the targeting instructions. You blew away the tubes with slugs. Depending on balance, that either froze it in place, or, more often, caused it to collapse in an untidy heap.

Either way, Buffy was using her gymnastic abilities to bounce off floor, walls, and ceiling while flaming. Winnie had never seen an Officer fight up close and personal like this, except Marine Officers. Marines of any rank were Marine before the rank. Just the way things were. As the monsters kept coming and Buffy kept calling targets, Winnie abstractly wondered what rank the Intelligence Officer was. Did she outrank Captain Mam? Wouldn't matter shipboard. No Marine ever took a ship command. If an Ensign was the senior naval Officer, he was Captain even if the ship also had a Marine General. Way of the world. Winnie kept roaring her battle songs and fighting her fight, guided by her Officer's commands. The tiny BarBee was a hell of a warrior. Winnie felt honored to fight by her side.

The fight ended with thirty or so of the constructs down and either charbroiled or melted. Winnie's suit had minor damage. Nothing she couldn't bench-repair back on ship. Armor repair was Winnie's type of tech. Winnie remotely felt the Officer returning the weapon and one unused grenade to the proper slots on Winnie's suit. Winnie knew Officers could take such liberties, but she still didn't LIKE it. Her kit was hers. The BarBee opened a recessed alcove in the corridor. Took out a med kit and spread healing foam over her singed hair and half her burned face. Winnie didn't trust foreign gear without testing, but Buffy had proven she knew her stuff. Came back with a tube of some quick-dry applique and told Winnie to use it on the weakened points in her smart armor—assured her it was compatible tech.

Meantime, Buffy went to another alcove. There was a suit. It should have been completely too large for her tiny body, but the BarBee clearly managed. Must be vocal commands that could make up for her feet and hands not fully filling the limbs. Must be interior straps to hold her in place. That was Officer-level knowledge. Buffy grabbed weapons off the dead constructs, then suddenly yelled, "DOWN!"

Winnie responded before she even realized she'd heard the word. Command voice. Huge flame roared through the corridor followed by a rush as the atmo vacated. "Katanga's at the data core. He just triggered the first traps. Past time to exit this junk heap before he blows it up." Winnie followed her Officer up the empty airless corridor to a set of blast doors. The BarBee worked the controls and it popped open. As soon as they were past it, she worked the controls from the other side, then refilled the section with atmo. The march resumed, Officer and Ranker.

Chapter 39

Katanga marveled that the data center showed zero damage. The BarBee had extreme skills to have been this selective in her destructiveness. He found an entry terminal, ignored the first prompt, and instead entered an elaborate 800-character code. Total gibberish, including custom glyphs that no user would know the system had. Eight hundred characters that dropped the user into the highest level of system admin access. One of several levels the end users didn't know existed. An 80-character code would be security overkill. The 800 was wildly beyond what other beings could attempt. It amused his kind to use such intricate barriers as proof of how far beyond evolution-designed primates they were. The idiot Reichers were fixated on physical objects. They bought the software. Bought from supposedly reliable suppliers. Suppliers who had been loyal for centuries. Suppliers who claimed they wrote the core programs themselves. Nope. Katanga's people made the original core software. Worked with chips and memory cores of amazing tech levels that came from even further out into the Deepest Beyond. His people had never been able to match those components, never able to reverse-engineer them. Nasty things happened when it was tried. Nasty, fatal things.

There were several levels of traps that shouldn't have been here, that no Reicher could access. Katanga triggered three and avoided over a dozen more. It left him shaken. There were levels beyond what he knew. Levels none of his diagnostics showed. He needed better equipment to find them. The precious hack was in there, but he wasn't going to find it here. Took him three minutes, but he found a supply sled with working antigrav. He loaded it with what should be the key components and memory stores, plus random pieces from the other arrays in case she'd cached her hack elsewhere.

The Hybrid Crew

He'd programmed in a set of codes labeling him and, by extension, the sled as friendly to the ship's internal defense expert systems. Friendly and senior officer status. The BarBee had hacked these also, but it had been a hasty hack. Nothing elegant. However, even a hasty showed a knowledge of the operating system that no one beyond Katanga's people was supposed to know was there. The ability to fool the ship's internal sensors and the expert system that ran them was a feature the Reichers did not even suspect existed. Had they known, they would have demanded control over it from the suppliers who functioned as middlemen.

Katanga didn't bother similarly protecting the others. He was no longer Katanga. He was again himself and no crewmate to any of them. It felt good to just be Gabriel. Now off to the courier and then home. Home needed what he had found more than it needed his message delivered. Their entire view of the universe was wrong, which had dangerous implications for their continued existence. A new Hijra might well be necessary. They had had many names and guises. Seemed like another might be coming. He chuckled at what the idiot Toymakers would do when their software supply line just abruptly died. It was a complex universe and few things were as they appeared, even on careful study.

Chapter 40

Captain Mam recalled some vague memories of the pseudo-centipede type of Toymaker construct. Seemed multiple lifetimes ago, the memories were so old and hazy. Probably back when she was a big-ship captain, bossed a squadron of them, before the politics of it all wearied her sufficiently to create a new persona as a Rimrunner captain. All of this bubbled on a secondary level. Her primary concern was her flamer, plus lobbing grenades. Meat fried and pseudo-plastic burned or melted. Every so often a segment threatened to overwhelm her and she had to resort to her multitool, using it as a club to beat some limbs into mush. Suits could be set for superhuman strength. Captain Mam knew how to get them beyond safe specs. There were operator code phrases to scream out. Smart officers learned this stuff. She'd always led her Marines on boarding actions. That wasn't Fleet protocol, but the very best big-ship captains learned that secret. To get the most out of your Marines, you had to lead them into battle, not just issue orders from the bridge.

As fast as she destroyed function in centipede sections, more slithered in. She felt herself being overwhelmed. Even the suit's many power features could not easily find firm footing in an ever-deepening pool of blood, machine oil, and other fluids. She stayed upright but with ever more precarious balance, which limited the leverage she could put into the swings of her club. The weight of segments on her was forcing her down, threatening to crush her and...and Ben came to the rescue. Laser in one hand, cutting away pseudo-life. The other hand firmly dragging her back, using the handhold every Marine suit had on the back for retrieval pickups. Once out from under the weight, Ben had clipped on the laser to his suit and begun tossing grenades to cover their retreat. He finally got her twenty meters beyond the prostrate head section of the centipede.

The "organism" seemed to have no central guiding brain. The rear kept trying to advance and failing to push forward the defunct head. So, it piled on itself, crushing the immobile van until it jammed the corridor. She and Ben turned their flamers to max and burned until the sections started exploding from boiling fluids. She switched to slugs, emptying hundred-round magazines one after another 'til she was sure nothing showed signs of life or motion. The bitch-bastard hybrid was dead and she was alive...and Ben had fallen over, his suit holed beyond the powers of his smart armor to cover. Shit! She checked command readouts and applied quick med procedures. It took minutes to stabilize him and if he didn't get back in the tanks he wouldn't live an hour. Where the fuck was Winnie?

Chapter 41

Winnie caught the last of the battle on her suit radio. Her Officer had given her a second frequency that both suits had, so she was able to tell Buffy of the need to up their pace. Buffy had Winnie send back a message to Captain Mam that they were six minutes out. Also, that Buffy knew where to find and how to use Reicher med nanites. The six minutes were mostly uneventful. Three more droids to fry, but they came in singletons. Buffy got two and Winnie the third. With an Officer along who knew Toymaker tech, Winnie found these were easy targets. It felt so good to be back under proper command. Winnie hadn't realized that Marine officers could also be Fleet Intelligence. Maybe the interface was via service in the Teams, the active attack force of Fleet Intelligence.

Intelligence had the Teams and Security had its Speznatz. Winnie had fought beside Team units before. Topnotch fighters. As good as Marines, even if the Teams thought they were better. Speznatz were just station bulls with fancy suits and attitude as far as Marines were concerned. Good enough for Federation Space and usually bright enough to stay inside the Line. Federation Space and even the Frontier were foreign universes to Winnie. The real world was the Diaspora, however far out into the Deep Beyond that ran. No one really knew. However far Fleet's patrols stretched, they kept finding scattered habitats, stations, ships, whole mud balls...humans or near-humans in all their varieties. Higher galactic 4 dimensional geography wasn't Winnie's strong suit, anyway.

Winnie was surprised to see Captain Mam react badly to Buffy. Wanted to argue rank, assert authority. Buffy was oblivious. She had contact codes and once a common frequency was agreed to so all the suits were on it, started shooting them into the airwaves at Captain Mam. Who clearly wasn't buying it. A standoff over rank and authorities while Ben died. Officers! Had to have them, but dumb as rocks.

Chapter 42

Holly Kim had recovered her breath. She was still working on recovering her nerve, but had progressed from terrified to merely frightened. She was in a data alcove with a gun in the bird's ear and shock manacles on his legs. Supposedly, he was entering permissions labeling the two of them as friendlies to the ship's defense systems and its droids. Supposedly. She'd made clear that any hint of treachery would cost his life. He had no reason to doubt her.

There had been a hell of a row between them once they had paused. He berated her for running away from the boat deck and the courier ship. Her escape had been less "away from" than not exactly straight toward that location, but she caught his meaning. She'd backhanded him and slapped the shock manacles on, then hit the shock button over and over until he was whimpering on the deck. She'd quizzed him again and again on whether he was really Fleet Security. He'd stuck with that story despite repeated shocks and laser burns. She'd even clipped off part of his beak with a knife and between screams he kept swearing he was Security. He wanted off this ship. He promised vast rewards if delivered to any good-sized Fleet base.

Holly had zero intention of going anywhere near a Fleet base. They would fry a Reicher ship, ignoring his recognition codes. No, she'd stop to get some of the money metals. Gold, platinum, palladium, silver...any of those or any combo would spend. A trolley load would suffice. No need to be greedy and no super rush. Aagney obviously had failed. Or, if he hadn't, Holly was already screwed and no helping it. Odds said no second courier to steal.

She wasn't trusting the bird's help while she tried to manage a ship this big. The bird had fucked Aagney and would do the same to her given the smallest chance. What she'd do is take the courier on a long set of jumps to a station she knew of that would let a ship with no IFF drift in the vicinity while everyone talked and trades were worked out. There was no Fleet Security agent there, or at least none that publicly fronted it. There was a ship's supplier who claimed he finked for Intelligence. He'd pay for the bird based on his codes. Orders of magnitude less than a Fleet base would pay, but no awkward questions, no peeling her mind deep enough to uncover things Captain Mam knew but hadn't disclosed to Fleet. The big payoff would be a Fleet-registered IFF. Would list her as friendly despite her ship silhouette. THAT would keep her alive until she'd gotten far enough away to buy a Merchanter ID and vanish. And go home. She could go home. It was a plan. Time to start.

Chapter 43

Bridgit Finnmark had once been a senior line officer. She hadn't liked the high-handed ways Fleet Intelligence commandeered assets then, and she certainly didn't like them now. She was prepared to buy that the BarBee was Fleet Intelligence. She'd take the assertion of rank as unproven. Bridgit didn't attach any probative value one way or the other to such assertions. These spooks often had dozens of personnel jackets claiming whatever rank was convenient. They lived in their own insular universe, more so when they copied themselves into extra bodies. The BarBee was obviously one such, as Fleet had not the first clue of how to hatch one. They didn't breed true or breed at all. Captain Mam couldn't for the life of her remember which, but there was a problem beyond Fleet's genetic tech base.

Part of why she accepted that the construct was probably an officer was that the ever-suspicious Winnie accepted her as such. Marines got recognition codes uploaded on a more current basis than ship or squadron commanders, who could consult machine memory in such situations. This Buffy was proving her worth now. Got Ben stripped out of his damaged suit. Smeared him with healing nanites and other quick fixes. Reichers were human enough, whatever their fantasies. Med tech that worked on them would work on Fleet personnel...or it was possible enough to be worth taking the BarBee's claims at face value. It wasn't as if there were alternatives to this. Maybe the Reicher stuff worked. Otherwise, he'd bleed out for sure.

As soon as Ben's breathing stabilized, Buffy went into a compartment and came out with a Reicher suit. She seemed to know the settings. The empty suit followed her, using its data system as a sort of instant droid work around. They gently arranged Ben in the suit and sealed it. The BarBee gave a series

The Hybrid Crew

of commands, part in Reicher speak and part a gibberish of alphanumerics. The suit on its own assumed its place in the line of march as the four of them started back to the docking port, back to the Rimrunner, back "home".

Chapter 44

The humanoid formerly known as Katanga Wa-Benzi arrived at the hanger bay pushing his grav sled. It was a huge chamber, easily a hundred meters high and several hundred meters long and wide. There were a variety of drones, shuttles, sleds, and scooters, but only three cradles for larger courier ships, of which only one was occupied. The jump-capable courier that was his destination and prize had droids of varying sizes and shapes swarming over it, doing last-minute preflight prep per the commands he had sent from the data center. All was in order...or so it appeared. The droids ignored him. This again fit his instructions. To them he was a senior officer.

He went straight to the main maintenance console, entered a different 800-character override code, and confirmed the preflight routines he'd sent instructions ahead from the main data center. The console confirmed the ship was almost finished being prepped for launch. Supplies had been loaded. So had four sleds of money metals. Most precious were three captured Merchanter IFFs and a Reicher one. Also, two blanks he could program later. Navigating the universe without an apparent ID could get fatal with amazing speed. Smart small ships kept multiples and lived on making lucky guesses of which to advertise when.

He keyed two droids, who took his sled of data stacks and parts. They would follow him aboard and see to storage. He'd be bringing a small squad of droids and constructs along as helpers. He didn't need them to fly the ship, or even to do EVA work, but... waste not, want not. The motto supposedly went back to Old Earth, Mudball #1.

It felt good to be Gabriel again, to be himself, to show his full powers and talents. He could play the masquerade, but it was not the fun game it was to some of his creche mates. He'd survived that round of culls, but not with the best marks. The breeding masters had made clear to him that his line was being kept for other talents. Talents like his abilities during jump. He lacked the piloting skills of a true witch, but he was quite good in the lesser skill range of the navigator. Jump space didn't coordinate well with real space. Things could pull you off course, sometimes badly. The true witch, the pilot level, could "steer" in jump, could compensate for this. A navigator couldn't manage that, but could notice the deviations. If they seemed too extreme, the navigator could drop his ship out of jump, back to real space, where the ship could be re-aimed for jump again. Jump was an art, not a science. His people had wasted centuries trying to get jump to make sense, but now even they, the true genetic supermen, mostly just accepted this as unknowable.

Enough ruminating. Gabriel sealed the lock behind him and made himself comfortable in the command chair. From there, he had the hanger opened to the void and eased his ship out of its cradle. He first keyed the intelligence running the cradle to swing it out of the ship and carefully disengage. The brain's sole function was this maneuver and, from its point of view, capture of an incoming courier was the hard maneuver. Easing one out was simple positional physics.

Once free of the cradle and adjacent to the battlecruiser's huge hull, he used careful short bursts of the atltitude jets to get away from the battlecruiser before switching to main reaction drive. He laughed at himself. It wasn't his ship. He was never going back. He could have hit the reaction drive once the cradle finished serving as a crane to move him partway out the open hanger door. It would have fried the hanger section, but...but he was a professional and there were ways one did and didn't do things. No need to be more of a barbarian than circumstances required. The universe had enough half-civilized chimps pretending to be intelligent lifeforms. He had no need to copy their juvenile carelessness.

Chapter 45

Holly Kim was within sight of the last doorway to the hangar bay when it slammed shut in front of her. Even on a big ship, she could feel the vibration as the air from that vast space voided and the cradle mechanism swung into action. She felt like filleting the bird for allowing this to happen. It would have felt SO good. Her next thought was to pull a really big grenade, hug the rescue ball she was dragging the bird in, and send them both to the nonexistent afterlife the Woglah-lovers prattled on about. Someplace where they could eat white raisins while fucking genemod sheep forever, or something like that. She's had a tame Woglah skypilot try to explain it to her one night in between hands of a poker game in the backroom of a dive bar. Those guys were not supposed to drink or gamble. He did both and justified it as being a modernized whatever-the-official-name of the cult was. She figured he could be a spotter for the bad-guy versions of his thing, but most station-dwellers sold info to anyone who was paying. Ship people hated stationers. Stationers hated ship people. Supposedly this went back to the original mud ball, to oasis folk versus caravan nomads. Whatever. Holly had never been a deep thinker. The universe was what it was. You adapted.

Right now, the needed adaption required the bird. She was still in atmo but the balls didn't carry sound well, so she keyed the speaker inside the bubble and laid reality out for the bird. He could help her find the bridge and take command of the repair droids, or she would start carving chunks off him to eat. He agreed to everything. He would. He'd try to backstab her later, but there was some slim chance she could barricade them into the command bridge, and make this work. She gave it one chance in a hundred. She detoured them through a Reicher armory first. She was stocking up on arms, ammo, and high-grade explosives. If birdman double-crossed her, that bridge was blowing up like a station hit with a high-v inert. Spectacular and beyond repair. Besides, if she got real lucky she'd have a battlecruiser to sell. It didn't have to be able to fight. Just move and jump. She'd never taken something this massive into jump. Normally, mass differences didn't matter much, but this big would be an adventure. That's it. She was having an adventure. If she kept thinking that way, she wouldn't collapse in terror and blow herself up to make it stop. Maybe. She hoped.

Holly realized she hadn't even asked which bridge Fritz was guiding her to. A ship this big would have two, maybe more. She laughed to herself. What did it matter? It was a bridge. She would rig a dead-man's switch. She'd get a battlecruiser or exit the universe with a bang, not a whimper. What more mattered? Her luck was so fucked at this point, odds said there was no way out. She'd made every move wrong since she set foot on this oversized hunk of metal. On reflection, there were worse things to be than a semi-slave on a Rimrunner. Pity she hadn't thought of that first. So, screw finding a bridge. Instead, she sliced open the rescue ball. Fritz was cowering, terrified. Good. Let him feel worse than she already did. She just pressed down the button on the shock controls and kept it down as Fritz died in convulsions. She cut a chunk off the corpse and tried to eat it. Tasted awful. She was in atmo in this corridor. Her last plan would work. She stopped chewing penguin, spat it out, and completed a circuit that converted herself into a military-grade fireball. Her last thought was that she was no longer afraid.

Chapter 46

Captain Mam was silent on the trip back to *Nantucket Prime*, and was grateful that Winnie and the BarBee were likewise. Bridgit was weighing options. Something smelled wrong with the BarBee. Too many coincidences. There was no way she could have anticipated a rescue. She knew too much. Too much about Reichers, too much about Fleet. Yet, Fleet Intelligence was a complex, baroque beast. Wheels within wheels, factions within factions. Multigenerational infiltration operations. Making sense out of the rabbit holes they dived into was beyond mere logic. Bridgit considered just making a brig out of a hanger bay supply locker and leaving the little pest confined in her Reicher power suit until *Nantucket Prime* could reach a Fleet base. The little construct had even offered this.

What decided Bridgit against this was Ben's condition. He needed to be put into the machines without delay. Kept on total rejuv support while the printers made him new organs and other parts. Yet, as Captain Mam, Bridgit had rigged reentry to the ship with numerous traps and barriers. All these would need time to disengage and dismantle. They would also need her to work without observation from Winnie or the BarBee. Even if she used a different pattern of defenses next time, allowing someone to learn her system would make foiling it easier. That was a risk she simply couldn't afford. Trust goes just so far. Even with Winnie.

Buffy and Winnie waited patiently on the sled until given the all-clear. The three of them got Ben to the med machines. With six hands, plus a med droid working, he was efficiently peeled out of the suit and properly situated in the main healing tank. Captain Mam saw to the machine settings while Buffy was a few meters over at the main med data station, inputting details of the nanites she had used on Ben. Somehow the pleasure construct knew tech detail on Reicher med nanites and emergency healing salves. Bridgit pegged that as another weirdness to be worked through when time permitted. Winnie was covering Buffy. Marine SOP with an unknown shipboard. Buffy was inputting steadily while singing some new silly tune, something about truth being lies. It sounded Old Earthy, but so did many types of music. It seemed to be in some antique dialect of Mercan.

Buffy finished her input two minutes or so before Bridgit and the droid finished the last processes for Ben. The monitor was rating his full recovery as "probable", but he was looking at nonrelativistic months in tank. Made Bridgit weigh for a second letting Buffy sit a crew station. It was a risk, but so was blind-jumping with a crew of only two. Bridgit was still debating when Buffy turned to Winnie. In an almost musical key, the BarBee said, "Deus vult." Without her suit language implants, Bridgit was clueless as to what the words meant. That became irrelevant when Winnie put her in a sleeper hold and she almost immediately lost consciousness.

Chapter 47

Bridgit felt that she was at the bottom of one of those long tube things that showed up in costume entertainments set on blue sky worlds. Sky at the top and water at the bottom. What were they called? Wells? Tells? Something like that. That guy named after the bar room concoction, Shakes Beer, had a few, she thought. It was all fuzzy and far away. Besides something important was happening. She was feeling expert taps from what must have been the ship's attitude jets. This was important somehow. Bridgit started swimming up the tube, as though one could have swum atmo in a low-grav section on a mud ball. Suddenly she was in the sky, only it wasn't sky, it was being mostly fully awake. Nothing she was seeing made sense. Winnie was strapped in to her post with the scan and weapons screens live. Buffy was piloting her ship. HER SHIP! What the fuck! Bridgit tried to stand and found herself expertly tied down to her command chair. Her screens were live, but her hands were constrained from reaching them to input commands. She tried verbal commands. The screens ignored her. She was frozen out.

Buffy chuckled and said, "Ah. You're awake. Good. Welcome to the rest of your life." Buffy's hands were manipulating the screens, working the attitude controls again before switching on the reaction engine. She was supplementing the screen commands with verbals.

Verbals that made no sense to Bridgit. Verbals that Buffy was obviously fluent in. Verbals that worked on a Fleet ship. "How?" Bridgit was now prepared to accept that maybe this construct was Fleet Intelligence after all.

"Oh, the Fleet Intelligence ID was valid...as far as that goes. We've been in that service since it was created. Fleet Intelligence was a composite from the beginning, back to when humans had barely left the mud ball they called Earth, the mother planet. A mix of nationals, corporates, and some other things everyone tried to pretend didn't exist. We're one of those bogymen of conspiracy tales. We were ancient even then. We'd been there long before the service we infiltrated back on planet was formed." The reaction drive started to slowly accelerate. Buffy had her vector and was starting the run-up to jump.

"Blind jump to where?" Bridgit needed data. Needed it badly.

"Not blind. I'm your jump and in-system pilot for now. I'm qualified as both. And don't worry about Winnie. She didn't turn on you. It's all planted hooks. Winnie, you may speak, but will not stop obeying my orders."

Winnie cursed a blue streak, but kept at her Officer's orders. Bridgit asked the obvious question. "How?"

"Hooks buried in the uploads every senior Noncom and Officer get. You seem lacking in them. Oh, well, no infil program works 100%. We don't use these often, but needs must this time. I'm late. Centuries late and at the wrong end of the spiral arm." Buffy saw the perplexed look on Bridgit's face. "It's a lot to take in at once. Take your time and digest it in pieces. I've got control of your ship. I've got control of you, Winnie, and Ben. I'm taking you someplace Beyond the Beyond in the truest sense. Oh, as you are putting the pieces together, chew on this one. Even the classified histories you had access to as a senior officer are absurd fantasies. Reality starts with this: humans didn't come from Earth. You're a successful colonization. There's so much more out there than Fleet knows." The BarBee read Bridgit's face as if she were telepathic. "Okay, believe I'm crazy. Doesn't matter. I'm going to take you further than you can imagine. Jump drive came from someplace. You're about to get a partial look at where. Oh, and the drive has higher gears than anyone inside Fleet space has puzzled out yet. So...I'm going to trank you down good and hard. We'll talk more nine jumps from now. By then, you'll be so far out in the Black that you'll never find your back without me. Ah, the adventures we're going to have."

As Bridgit watched in horror, one of the med droids rolled in and gave her the trank shot. As she faded, she could hear the BarBee singing about being "Bound for Glory".

www.ingramcontent.com/pod-product-compliance
Lightning Source LLC
Chambersburg PA
CBHW031031190726
48286CB00003BA/1120